He was expected to laugh, but it was taking all his concentration just to breathe because she'd forgotten not to look at him.

And then he could see that it wasn't just him. They were both struggling with the zing of lightning that arced between them.

'Since Plan B was a threat to sue me for malicious damage…'

Her voice was thick, her pupils huge against the shot-silk blue. What would she do if he reached out and took her hand and held it against his zip? If he sucked her lower lip into his mouth?

'…I didn't think there was much point in hanging around.'

He turned away and crossed to the kettle, picking it up to make sure there was some water in it before switching it on. Any distraction from the thoughts racketing through his head. The same thoughts that had driven him from her office amplified a hundred times.

He had no problem with lust at first sight. With uncomplicated, life's-too-short sex that gave everyone a good time and didn't screw with your head. This was complicated with knobs on. He should never have let her stay.

But he could not have sent her away…

Dear Reader

I'm absolutely thrilled to be able to bring you FOR HIS EYES ONLY in the iconic blue covers of the Modern Tempted™ series.

One of the joys of writing is research, and the setting for Hadley Chase was inspired by a visit to historic Ashdown House, where my guide was historical novelist Nicola Cornick. It's on the Wiltshire/Berkshire borders, set in beautiful downland, and Charles II and Prince Rupert went there to hunt and have a good time. The house at Hadley Chase was a gift after a visit to Great Chalfield Manor, just down the road from my home. Gorgeous scenery, lovely gardens and brilliant fun.

It was enormous fun to stretch myself a little in new directions, too, and I hope you'll enjoy getting to know Natasha Gordon and Darius Hadley as much as they enjoy getting to know one another! If you'd like to see some of my inspiration for the book, do come and take a look at their 'board' at Pinterest.

All love

Liz

FOR HIS EYES ONLY

BY
LIZ FIELDING

Published in Great Britain 2014
by Mills & Boon, an imprint of Harlequin (UK) Limited,
Eton House, 18-24 Paradise Road, Richmond, Surrey, TW9 1SR

© 2014 Liz Fielding

ISBN: 978 0 263 24193 8

Harlequin (UK) Limited's policy is to use papers that are natural,
renewable and recyclable products and made from wood grown in
sustainable forests. The logging and manufacturing processes conform
·igin.

Liz Fielding was born with itchy feet. She made it to Zambia before her twenty-first birthday and, gathering her own special hero and a couple of children on the way, lived in Botswana, Kenya and Bahrain—with pauses for sightseeing pretty much everywhere in between. She finally came to a full stop in a tiny Welsh village cradled by misty hills, and these days mostly leaves her pen to do the travelling.

When she's not sorting out the lives and loves of her characters she potters in the garden, reads her favourite authors, and spends a lot of time wondering, *What if...?*

For news of upcoming books—and to sign up for her occasional newsletter—visit Liz's website: www.lizfielding.com

This and other titles by Liz Fielding are available in eBook format from www.millsandboon.co.uk

DEDICATION

With thanks to Kate Hardy and Caroline Anderson
for their never-failing belief.

And to Gail McCurry Waldrep for the fudge frosting.

CHAPTER ONE

'WHAT'S GOT MILES'S knickers in a twist?' Natasha Gordon poured herself half a cup of coffee. Her first appointment had been at eight and she'd been on the run ever since. She had to grab any opportunity to top up her caffeine level. 'I was on my way to a viewing at the St John's Wood flat when I got a message to drop everything and come straight back here.'

Janine, Morgan and Black's receptionist and always the first with any rumour, lifted her slender cashmere-clad shoulders in a don't-ask-me shrug. 'If that's what he said, you'd better not keep him waiting,' she said, but, shrug notwithstanding, the ghost of an I-know-something-you-don't smile tugged at lips on which the lipstick was always perfectly applied.

Tash abandoned the untouched coffee and headed for the stairs, taking them two at a time. Miles Morgan, senior partner of Morgan and Black, first port of call for the wealthy flooding into London from all corners of the world to snap up high-end real estate, had been dropping heavy hints for weeks that the vacant 'associate' position was hers.

Damn right. She'd worked her socks off for the last three years and had earned that position with hard work and long hours and Janine, who liked everyone to know how 'in' she was with the boss, had casually let slip the news on Friday afternoon that he would be spending the weekend in the country with the semi-retired 'Black' to discuss the future of the firm.

'Down, pulse, down,' she muttered, pausing outside his office to scoop up a wayward handful of hair and anchor it in place with great-grandma's silver clip.

She always started out the day looking like a career woman on the up, but haring about London all morning had left her more than a little dishevelled and things had begun to unravel. Her hair, her make-up, her shirt.

She tucked in her shirt and was checking the top button when the door opened.

'Janine! Is she here yet?' Miles shouted before he realised she was standing in front him. 'Where the hell have you been?'

'I had a viewing at the Chelsea house first thing,' she said, used to his short fuse. 'They played it very close to their chests, but the wife's eyes were lit up like the Blackpool illuminations. I guarantee they'll make an offer before the end of the day.'

The prospect of a high five-figure commission would normally be enough to change his mood but he merely grunted and the sparkle of anticipation went flat. Whatever Janine had been smiling about, it wasn't the prospect of the office party Miles would throw to celebrate the appointment of the new associate.

'It's been non-stop since then,' she added, and it wasn't going to ease up this side of six. 'Is this urgent, Miles? I'm showing Glencora Jarrett the St John's Wood apartment in half an hour and the traffic is solid.'

'You can forget that. I've sent Toby.'

'Toby?' Her occasionally significant other had been on a rugby tour in Australia and wasn't due home until the end of the month. She shook her head. It wasn't important, but Lady Glen… 'No, she specifically asked—'

'For you. I know, but a viewing isn't a social engagement,' he cut in before she could remind him that Lady Glencora was desperately nervous and would not go into an unoccupied apartment with a male negotiator.

'But—'

'Forget Her Ladyship,' he said, thrusting the latest edition of the *Country Chronicle* into her hands. 'Take a look at this.'

The magazine was open at the full-page advertisement for Hadley Chase, a historic country house that had just come on the market.

'Oh, that came out really well...' A low mist, caught by the rising sun, had lent the house a golden, soft-focus enchantment that hid its many shortcomings. Well worth the effort of getting up at the crack of dawn and driving into the depths of Berkshire on the one day in the week that she could have had a lie-in. 'The phone will be ringing off the hook,' she said, offering it back to him.

'Read on,' he said, not taking it.

'I know what it says, Miles. I wrote it.' The once grand house was suffering from age and neglect and she'd focused on the beauty and convenience of the location to tempt potential buyers to come and take a look. 'You approved it,' she reminded him.

'I didn't approve this.'

She frowned. Irritable might be his default mode but, even for Miles, this seemed excessive. Had some ghastly mistake slipped past them both? It happened, but this was an expensive full-page colour ad, and she'd gone over the proof with a fine-tooth comb. Confident that nothing could have gone wrong, she read out her carefully composed copy.

'"A substantial seventeenth-century manor house in a sought-after location on the Berkshire Downs within easy reach of motorway links to London, the Midlands and the West. That's the good news. The bad news..."' She faltered. Bad news? What the...?

'Don't stop now.'

The words were spoken with a clear, crisp, don't-argue-with-me certainty, but not by her boss, and she spun around as the owner of the voice rose from the high-backed leather armchair set in front of Miles Morgan's desk and turned to face her.

Her first impression was of darkness. Dark hair, dark clothes, dark eyes in a mesmerising face that missed beauty by a hair's breadth, although a smile might have done the business.

The second was of strength. There was no bulk, but his shoulders were wide beneath a crumpled linen jacket so old that the black had faded to grey, his abdomen slate-flat under a T-shirt that hung loosely over narrow hips.

His hand was resting on the back of the chair, long calloused fingers curled over the leather. They were the kind of fingers that she could imagine doing unspeakable things to her. Was imagining…

She looked up and met eyes that seemed to penetrate every crevice, every pore, and a hot blush, beginning somewhere low in her belly, spread like wildfire in every direction—

'Natasha!'

Miles's sharp interjection jolted her back to the page but it was a moment before she could catch her breath, gather her wits and focus on the words dancing in front of her.

…the bad news is the wet rot, woodworm, crumbling plasterwork and leaking roof. The vendor would no doubt have preferred to demolish the house and re-develop the land, but it's a Grade II listed building in the heart of the Green Belt so he's stuffed. There is a fine oak Tudor staircase but, bearing in mind the earlier reference to wet rot and woodworm, an early viewing is advised if you want to see the upper floors.

Her heart still pounding with the shock of a sexual attraction so powerful that she was trembling, she had to read it twice before it sank in. And when it did her pulse was still in a sorry state.

'I don't understand,' she said. Then, realising how feeble that sounded, 'How did this happen?'

'How, indeed?'

Her question had been directed at Miles, but the response came from Mr Tall, Dark and Deadly. Who *was* he?

'Hadley,' he said, apparently reading her mind. Or maybe she'd asked the question out loud. She needed to get a grip. She needed an ice bath...

She cleared her throat. 'Hadley?' His name still emerged as if spoken by a surprised frog, but that wasn't simply because all her blood had apparently drained from her brain to the more excitable parts of her anatomy. The house was unoccupied and the sale was being handled by the estate's executors and, since no one had mentioned a real-life, flesh-and-blood Hadley, she'd assumed the line had run dry.

'Darius Hadley,' he elaborated, clearly picking up on her doubt.

In her career she'd worked with everyone, from young first-time buyers scraping together a deposit, to billionaires investing in London apartments and town houses costing millions. She knew that appearances could be deceptive but Darius Hadley did not have the look of a man whose family had been living in the Chase since the seventeenth century, when a grateful Charles II had given the estate to one James Hadley, a rich merchant who'd funded him in exile.

With the glint of a single gold earring amongst the mass of black curls tumbling over his collar, the crumpled linen jacket faded from black to grey, jeans worn threadbare at the knees, he looked more like a gypsy, or a pirate. Perhaps that was where the Hadley fortune had come from—plundering the Spanish Main with the likes of Drake. Or, with the legacy now in the hands of a man bearing the name of a Persian king, it was possible that his ancestors had chosen to travel east overland, to trade in silk and spices.

This man certainly had the arrogance to go with his name but, unlike his forebears, it seemed that he had no interest in settling down to live the life of a country gentleman. Not that she blamed him for that.

Hadley Chase, with roses growing over its timbered Tudor heart, might look romantic in the misty haze of an early summer sunrise, but it was going to take a lot of time and a very deep purse to bring it up to modern expectations in plumbing, heating and weatherproofing. There was nothing romantic about nineteen-fifties plumbing and, from the neglected state of both house and grounds, it was evident that the fortune needed to maintain it was long gone.

On the bright side, even in these cash-strapped days, there were any number of sheikhs, pop stars and Russian oligarchs looking for the privacy of a country estate no more than a helicopter hop from the centre of London and she was looking forward to adding the Chase to her portfolio of sales in the very near future. She had big plans for the commission.

Miles cleared his throat and she belatedly stuck out her hand.

'Natasha Gordon. How d'you do, Mr Hadley?'

'I've been stuffed, mounted and hung out to dry,' he replied. 'How do you think I feel?' he demanded, ignoring her hand.

'Angry.' He had every right to be angry. Hell, she was furious with whoever had meddled with her carefully worded description and they would feel the wrath of her tongue when she found out who it was, but that would have to wait. Right now she had to get a grip of her hormones, be totally professional and reassure him that this wasn't the disaster it appeared. 'I don't know what happened here, Mr Hadley, but I promise you it's just a minor setback.'

'A minor setback?' Glittering eyes—forget charcoal, they were jet—skewered her to the floor and Tash felt the heat rise up her neck and flood her cheeks. She was blushing. He'd made her blush with just a look. That was outrageous... 'A *minor* setback?' he repeated, with the very slightest emphasis on 'minor'.

His self-control was impressive.

Okaaay... She unpeeled her tongue from the roof of her mouth, snatched in a little oxygen to get her brain started and said, 'Serious purchasers understand that there will be problems with this type of property, Mr Hadley.'

'They expect to be able to view the upper floors without endangering their lives,' he pointed out. He hadn't raised his voice; he didn't have to. He'd made his point with a quiet, razor-edged precision that made Miles's full-blown irritation look like a toddler tantrum.

'Natasha!' Miles prompted, more sharply this time. 'Have you got something to say to Mr Hadley?'

'What?' She dragged her gaze from the seductive curve of Darius Hadley's lower lip and fixed it somewhere around his prominent Adam's apple, which only sent her mind off on another, even more disturbing direction involving extremities.

Do not look at his feet!

'Oh, um, yes...' She'd tried desperately to get her brain in gear, recall the notes she'd made, as she stared at scuffed work boots, jeans smeared with what looked like dry grey mud and clinging to powerful thighs. He'd obviously dropped whatever he was doing and come straight to the office when he'd seen the ad. Did he work on a building site? 'Actually,' she said, 'there's more than one set of stairs so it isn't a problem.'

'And that's your professional opinion?'

'Not that I recall there being anything wrong with the main staircase that a thorough seeing to with a vacuum cleaner wouldn't fix,' she added hurriedly when Miles sounded as if he might be choking. Come on, Tash…this is what you do. 'I did advise the solicitor handling the sale that they should get in a cleaning contractor to give the place a good bottoming.'

A muscle tightened in his jaw. 'And what was their response to that?'

'They said they'd get the caretaker to give it a once-over.'

Some property owners did nothing to help themselves, but this probably wasn't the moment to say so.

'So it's just the woodworm, rot and missing lead flashing on the roof that a potential buyer has to worry about?' Darius Hadley raised his dark brows a fraction of a millimetre and every cell in her body followed as if he'd jerked a string.

Amongst a jangle of mixed messages—her head urging her to take a step back, every other part of her wanting to reach out and touch—she just about managed to stand her ground.

'Actually,' she said, 'according to the paperwork, the woodworm was treated years ago.' Something he would have known if he'd taken the slightest interest in the house he'd apparently inherited. 'I think you'll find that it's the cobwebs that will have women running screaming—'

Behind Hadley's back, Miles made a sharp mouth-zipped gesture. 'Mr Hadley isn't looking for excuses. What he's waiting for,' he said, 'what he's *entitled* to, is an explanation and an apology.'

She frowned. Surely Miles had already covered that ground? She assumed she'd been called in to discuss a plan of action.

'Don't bother; I've heard enough,' Hadley said before

she could get in a word. 'You'll be hearing from my lawyer, Morgan.'

'Lawyer?' What use was a lawyer going to be? 'No, really—'

Darius Hadley cut off her protest with a look that froze her in mid-sentence and seemed to go on for an eternity. Lethal eyes, a nose bred for looking down, a mouth made for sin... Finally, satisfied that he'd silenced her, his eyes seemed to shimmer, soften, warm to smoky charcoal and then, as she took half a step towards him, he nodded at Miles and walked out of the office, leaving the room ringing with his presence. Leaving her weak to the bone.

She put out a hand to grasp the back of the chair he'd been sitting in. It was still warm from his touch and the heat seemed to travel up her arm and spread through her limbs, creating little sparks throughout her body, igniting all the erogenous zones she was familiar with and quite a few that were entirely new.

Phew. Double phewy-phew...

'He's a bit tense, isn't he?' she said shakily. A sleek, dark Dobermann to Toby's big, soft Labrador puppy—to be approached with caution rather than a hug. But the rewards if you won his trust...

Forget it! A man like that wasn't a keeper. All you could hope for was to catch his attention for a moment. But what a moment—

'With good reason,' Miles said, interrupting a chain of thought that was going nowhere. Dark, brooding types had never been even close to the top of her list of appealing male stereotypes. Far too high-maintenance. *Rude* dark, brooding types had never figured.

A barrage of hoots from the street below distracted her, but there was no escape there. Apparently oblivious to the traffic, Darius Hadley was crossing the street and several people stopped to watch him stride down the road in the direction of Sloane Square. Most of them were women.

It wasn't just her, then.

Without warning he stopped, swung round and looked up at the window where she was standing as if he'd known she'd be there. And she forgot to breathe.

'Natasha!'

She jumped, blinked and when she looked again he'd gone and for a moment she was afraid that he was coming back. Hoped that he was coming back, but a moment later he reappeared further along the street and she turned her back on the window before he felt her eyes boring into the back of his head and turned again to catch her looking.

'Have you spoken to the *Chronicle*?' she asked; anything to distract herself.

'The first thing I did when Mr Hadley's solicitor contacted me early this morning was to call the *Chronicle*'s advertising manager.' Miles walked across to his desk and removed a sheet of paper from a file and handed it to her. 'He sent this over from his office. Hadley hasn't seen it yet but it's only a matter of time before his lawyer contacts them.'

It was a photocopied proof of the ad for Hadley Chase— exactly as she'd read it out—complete with a tick next to the 'approved' box and her signature scrawled across the bottom.

'No, Miles. This is wrong.' She looked up. 'This isn't what I signed.'

'But you did write that,' he insisted.

'One or two of the phrases sound vaguely familiar,' she admitted.

She sometimes wrote a mock advertisement describing a property in the worst possible light when she thought it would help the vendor to see the property through the eyes of a potential buyer. The grubby carpet in the hall, the children's finger marks on the doors, the tired kitchen. Stuff that wouldn't cost much to fix, but would make all the difference to the prospects of a sale.

'Oh, come on, Tash. It sounds exactly like one of your specials.'

'My "specials" have the advantage of being accurate. And helpful.'

'So you would have mentioned the leaking roof?'

'Absolutely. Damaged ceilings and pools of water are about as off-putting as it gets,' she said, hating that she was on the defensive when she hadn't done anything wrong.

'What about the stairs?'

'I'm sure they'd be lovely if you could see them for the dust and dead leaves that blew in through a broken window.' The house had been empty since the last occupant had been moved to a nursing home when Alzheimer's had left him a danger to himself a couple of years ago. 'The caretaker is worse than useless. I had to find some card and fill the gap myself but it's just a temporary solution. The first serious gust of wind will blow it out. And, frankly, if I were Darius Hadley I'd put a boot up the backside of the estate executor because he's no help.' He didn't reply. 'Come on, Miles. You know I didn't send this to the *Chronicle*.'

'Are you sure about that? Really? We all know that you've been putting in long hours. What time was your first viewing this morning?'

'Eight, but—'

'What time did you finish last night?' He didn't wait for her to answer but consulted a printout of her diary, no doubt supplied by Janine. No wonder she'd been smiling. This was much more fun than an office party. Gossip city… 'Your last viewing was at nine-thirty so you were home at what? Eleven? Eleven-thirty?'

It had been after midnight. Buyers couldn't always fit into a tidy nine-till-five slot. Far from complaining about the extra hours she put in, that they all put in—with the exception of Toby, who never allowed anything to interfere with rugby training, took time off whenever he felt like it and got away with murder because his great-aunt was married to Peter Black—Miles expected it.

'They flew from the States to view that apartment. I could hardly tell them that I finished at five-thirty,' she pointed out. They'd come a long way and wanted to see every detail and she wasn't about to rush them.

'No one can keep up that pace for long without something suffering,' he replied, not even bothering to ask if they were likely to make an offer. 'It seems obvious to me that you attached the wrong document when you emailed your copy to the *Chronicle.*'

'No—'

'I blame myself.' He shook his head. 'I've pushed you too hard. I should have seen it coming.'

Seen *what* coming?

'I didn't attach the wrong anything,' she declared, fizzing with indignation, her pulse still racing but with anger now rather than anticipation. How dared anyone tamper with her carefully composed ad? 'And even if I had made a mistake, don't you think I'd have noticed it when the proof came back?'

'If you'd actually had time to look at it.'

'I made time,' she declared. 'I checked every word. And what the hell was the *Chronicle* thinking? Why didn't someone on the advertising desk query it?'

'They did.' He glanced at the ad. 'They called this office on the twentieth. Unsurprisingly, they made a note for their records.'

'Okay, so which idiot did they speak to?'

He handed her the page so that she could see for herself. 'An idiot by the name of Natasha Gordon.'

'No!'

'According to the advertising manager, you assured them that it was the latest trend, harking back fifty years to an estate agent famous for the outrageous honesty of his advertisements.' His tone, all calm reason, raised the small hairs on the back of her neck. Irritable, she could handle. This was just plain scary. 'Clearly, you were angry with the executors for not taking your advice.'

'If they didn't have the cash, they didn't have the cash, although I imagine their fees are safely in the bank. Believe me, if I'd been aping the legendary Roy Brooks, I'd have made a far better job of it than this,' she said, working hard to sound calm even while her pulse was going through the roof. 'There was plenty to work with. No one from the *Chronicle* talked to me.' Calm, cool, professional...

'So what are you saying? That the advertising manager of the *Chronicle* is lying? Or that someone pretended to be you? Come on, Tash, who would do that?' he asked. 'What would anyone have to gain?'

She swallowed. Put like that, it did sound crazy.

'You are right about one thing, though,' he continued. 'The phone has been ringing off the hook—' her sigh of relief came seconds too soon '—but not with people desperate to view Hadley Chase. They are all gossip columnists and the editors of property pages wanting a comment.'

She frowned. 'Already? The magazine has been on the shelves for less than two hours.'

'You know what they say about bad news.' He took the ad from her and tossed it onto his desk. 'In this instance I imagine it was given a head start by someone working at the *Chronicle* tipping them off.'

'I suppose. How did Darius Hadley hear about it?'

'I imagine the estate executors received the same phone calls.'

She shook her head, letting the problem of how this had happened go for the moment and concentrating instead on how to fix it. 'The one thing I do know is that there's no such thing as bad publicity. I meant what I said to Mr Hadley. Handled right...'

'For heaven's sake, Tash, you've made both the firm and Mr Hadley into a laughing stock. There is no way to handle this "right"! He's withdrawn the house from the market and, on top of the considerable expenses we've already incurred, we're not only facing a hefty claim for damages from Hadley but irreparable damage to the Morgan and Black name.'

'All of which will go away if we find a buyer quickly,' she insisted, 'and it's going to be all over the weekend property pages.'

'I'm glad you realise the extent of the problem.'

'No...' She'd run a Google search when Hadley Chase had been placed in their hands for sale. There was nothing like a little gossip, a bit of scandal to garner a few column inches in one of the weekend property supplements. Unfortunately, despite her speculation on the source of their wealth, the Hadleys had either been incredibly discreet or dull beyond imagining. She'd assumed the latter; if James Hadley had been an entertaining companion, his money would have earned him a lot more than a smallish estate in the country. He'd have been given a title and a place at Charles II's court.

Darius Hadley had blown that theory right out of the water.

Forget his clothes. With his cavalier curls, his earring, the edge of something dangerous that clung to him like a shadow, he would have been right at home there. Her fingers twitched as she imagined what it would be like to run her fingers through those silky black curls, over his flat abs.

She curled them into her palms, shook off the image—this wasn't about Darius Hadley; it was about his house.

'Come on, Miles,' she said. 'You couldn't buy this kind of publicity. The house is in a fabulous location and buyers with this kind of money aren't going to be put off by problems you'll find in any property of that age.' Well, not much. 'I'll make some calls, talk to a few people.' Apparently speaking to a brick wall, she threw up her hands. 'Damn it, I'll go down to Hadley Chase and take a broom to the place myself!'

'You'll do nothing, talk to no one,' he snapped.

'But if I can find a buyer quickly—'

'Stop! Stop right there.' Having shocked her into silence, he continued. 'This is what is going to happen. I've booked you into the Fairview Clinic—'

'The *Fairview*?' A clinic famous for taking care of celebrities with drug and drink problems?

'We'll issue a statement saying that you're suffering from stress and will be having a week or two of complete rest under medical supervision.'

'No.' Sickness, hospitals—she'd had her fill of them as a child and nothing would induce her to spend a minute in one without a very good reason.

'The firm's medical plan will cover it,' he said, no doubt meaning to reassure her.

'No, Miles.'

'While you're recovering,' he continued, his voice hardening, 'you can consider your future.'

'Consider my future?' Her future was stepping up to an associate's office, not being hidden away like some soap star with an alcohol problem until the dust cleared. 'You've got to be kidding, Miles. This has to be a practical joke that's got out of hand. There's a juvenile element in the front office that needs a firm—'

'What I need,' he said, each word given equal weight, 'is for you to cooperate.'

He wasn't listening, she realised. Didn't want to hear what she had to say. Miles wasn't interested in how this had happened, only in protecting his firm's reputation. He needed a scapegoat, a fall guy, and it was her signature on the ad.

That was why he'd summoned her back to the office— to show the sacrifice to Darius Hadley. Unsurprisingly, he hadn't been impressed. He didn't want the head of some apparently witless woman who stammered and blushed when he looked at her. He was going for damages so Miles was instituting Plan B—protecting the firm's reputation by destroying hers.

She was in trouble.

'I've spoken to Peter Black and he's discussed the situation with our lawyers. We're all agreed that this is the best solution,' Miles continued, as if it was a done deal.

'Already?'

'There was no time to waste.'

'Even so… What kind of lawyer would countenance such a lie?'

'What lie?' he enquired blandly. 'Burnout happens to the best of us.'

Burnout? She was barely simmering, but the lawyers— covering all eventualities—probably had the press statement drafted and ready to go. She would be described as a 'highly valued member of staff'…blah-de-blah-de-blah… who, due to work-related stress, had suffered a 'regrettable' breakdown. All carefully calculated to give the impression that she'd been found gibbering into her keyboard.

It would, of course, end with everyone wishing her a speedy return to health. Miles was clearly waiting for her to do the decent thing and take cover in the Fairview so that he could tell them to issue it. The clinic's reputation for keeping their patients safe from the lenses of the paparazzi, safe from the intrusion of the press, was legendary.

Suddenly she wasn't arguing with him over the best way to recover the situation, but clinging to the rim of the basin by her fingernails as her career was being flushed down the toilet.

'This is wrong,' she protested, well aware that the decision had already been made, that nothing she said would change that. 'I didn't do this.'

'I'm doing my best to handle a public relations nightmare that you've created, Natasha.' His voice was flat, his face devoid of expression. 'It's in your own best interests to cooperate.'

'It's in yours,' she retaliated. 'I'll be unemployable. Unless, of course, you're saying that I'll be welcomed back with open arms after my rest cure? That my promotion to associate, the one you've been dangling in front of me for months, is merely on hold until I've recovered?'

'I have to think of the firm. The rest of the staff,' he said with a heavy sigh created to signal his disappointment with her. 'Please don't be difficult about this.'

'Or what?' she asked.

'Tash... Please. Why won't you admit that you made a mistake? That you're fallible...sick; everyone—maybe even Mr Hadley—will sympathise with you, with us.'

He was actually admitting it!

'I didn't do this,' she repeated but, even to her own ears, she was beginning to sound like the little girl who, despite the frosting around her mouth, had refused to own up to eating two of the cupcakes her mother had made for a charity coffee morning.

'I'm sorry, Natasha, but if you refuse to cooperate we'll have no choice but to dismiss you without notice for bringing the firm into disrepute.' He took refuge behind his desk before he added, 'If you force us to do that we will, of course, have no option but to counter-sue you for malicious damage.'

Deep, deep trouble.

'I'm not sick,' she replied, doing her best to keep her voice steady, fighting down the scream of outrage that was beginning to build low in her belly. 'As for the suit for damages, I doubt either you or Mr Hadley would get very far with a jury. While the advertisement may not have been what he signed up for—' she was being thrown to the wolves, used as a scapegoat for something she hadn't done and she had nothing to lose '—it's the plain unvarnished truth.'

'Apart from the woodworm and the stairs,' he reminded her stonily.

'Are you prepared to gamble on that?' she demanded. 'Who knows what's under all that dirt?'

She didn't wait for a response. Once your boss had offered you a choice between loony and legal action, any meaningful dialogue was at an end.

CHAPTER TWO

How DARED HE? How bloody dared he even suggest she might be suffering from stress, burnout? Damn it, Miles had to know this was all a crock of manure.

Tash, despite her stand-up defiance, was shaking as she left Miles Morgan's office and she headed for the cloakroom. There was no way she could go downstairs and face Janine, who'd obviously known exactly what was coming, until she had pulled herself together.

She jabbed pins in her hair, applied a bright don't-care-won't-care coating of lipstick and some mental stiffeners to her legs before she attempted the stairs she'd run up with such optimism only a few minutes earlier.

She'd been ten minutes, no more, but Janine was waiting with a cardboard box containing the contents of her desk drawers.

'Everything's there,' she said, not the slightest bit embarrassed. On the contrary, the smirk was very firmly in place. They'd never been friends but, while she'd never given Janine a second thought outside the office, it was possible that Janine—behind the faux sweetness and the professional smile and ignoring the hours she put in, her lack of a social life—had resented her bonuses. 'It's mostly rubbish.'

She didn't bother to answer. She could see for herself that the contents of her desk drawers had been tipped into the box without the slightest care.

Janine was right; it was mostly rubbish, apart from a spare pair of tights, the pencil case that one of her brothers had given her and the mug she used for her pens. She picked it up and headed for the door.

'Wait! Miles said…'

In her opinion, Miles had said more than enough but, keeping her expression impassive, she turned, waited.

'He asked me to take your keys.'

Of course he had. He wouldn't want her coming back when the office was closed to prove what havoc she could really cause, given sufficient provocation. Fortunately for him, her reputation was more important to her than petty revenge.

She put down the box, took out her key ring, removed the key to the back door of the office and handed it over without a word.

'And your car keys,' she said.

Until that moment none of this had seemed real, but the BMW convertible had been the reward Miles had dangled in front of his staff for anyone reaching a year-end sales target that he had believed impossible. She'd made it with a week to spare and it was her pride and joy as well as the envy of every other negotiator in the firm. Could someone have done this to her just to get…?

She stopped. That way really did lie madness.

No doubt Miles would use those spectacular sales figures to back up his claim of 'burnout', suggesting she'd driven herself to achieve the impossible and prove that she was better than anyone else. *So very sad…*

He might even manage to squeeze out a tear.

All he'd have to do was think of the damages he'd have to pay Darius Hadley.

Taking pride in the fact that her fingers weren't shaking—it was just the rest of her, apparently—she removed the silver Tiffany key ring Toby had bought her for Christmas from her car keys and dropped it in her pocket, but she held on to the keys. 'I'll clear my stuff out of the back.'

'I'll come with you,' Janine said, following her to the door. 'I need to make sure it's locked up safely.'

She wasn't trusted to hand over the keys? Or did the wretched woman think she'd drive off in it? Add car theft to her crimes? Oh, wait. She was supposed to be crazy...

'Actually, you'll need to do more than that. I'm parked in a twenty-minute zone and it'll need moving before— Oh, too late...'

She startled the traffic warden slapping a ticket on the windscreen with a smile before clicking the lock and tossing the keys to Janine as if she didn't give a fig. She wouldn't give her the pleasure of telling everyone how she'd crumpled, broken down. It was just a car. She'd have it back in no time. Just as soon as Miles stopped panicking and started thinking straight.

She emptied the glovebox, gathered her wellington boots, the ancient waxed jacket she'd bought in a charity shop and her umbrella and added them to the box, then reached for her laptop bag.

'I'll take that.'

'My laptop?' She finally turned to look at Janine. 'Did Miles ask you to take it?'

'He's got a lot on his mind,' she replied with a little toss of her head. In other words, no.

'True, and when I find out who's responsible for this mess he won't be the only one. In the meantime,' she said, hooking the strap over her shoulder and patting the soft leather case that held her precious MacBook Pro, 'if he should ask for it, I suggest you remind him that I bought it out of my January bonus.'

Janine, caught out, flushed bright pink but it was a short-lived triumph.

'There's a taxi waiting to take you to the Fairview,' she said, turning on her heel and heading back to the office.

Tash glanced at the black cab, idling at the kerb. Even loaded as she was, the temptation to stalk off in the direction of the nearest Underground station was strong, but there was no one apart from the traffic warden to witness the gesture so she climbed aboard and gave him her address.

The driver looked back. 'I was booked for the Fairview.'

'I have to go home first,' she said, straight-faced. 'I'm going to need a nightie and toothbrush.'

Darius strode the length of the King's Road, fury and the need to put distance between himself and Natasha Gordon driving his feet towards the Underground.

A minor setback? A house that she'd made unsellable, and a seven-figure tax bill on a house he couldn't live in—what would merit serious bother in her eyes?

Cornflower-blue, with hair that looked as if she'd just tumbled out of bed and a figure that was all curves. Sexy as hell, which was where his thoughts were taking him.

Once on the train, he took out the small sketchbook he carried with him and did what he had always done when he wanted to block out the world. He drew what he saw. Not the interior of the train, the woman sitting opposite him, the baby sleeping on her lap, but what was in his head.

Dark, angry images that had been stirred up by a house he'd never wanted to set foot in again but just refused to let go. But that wasn't what appeared on the page. His hand, ignoring his head, was drawing Natasha Gordon. Her eyes, startled wide as he'd confronted her. The way her brow had arched like the wing of a kestrel hovering over a hedge-row, waiting for an unsuspecting vole to make a move. The curve of hair drooping from an antique silver clasp, the tiny crease at the corner of her mouth that had appeared when

she'd offered him a smile along with her hand. It was as
if her image had burned itself into his brain, every detail
pinpoint-sharp. The blush heating her cheeks, a fine chain
about her neck that disappeared between invitingly generous breasts. Her long legs.

Was he imagining them?

He couldn't remember looking at her legs and yet he'd
drawn her shoes—black suede, dangerously high heels, a
sexy little ankle strap…

He did not fight it, but drew obsessively, continuously,
as if by putting her on paper he could clear his mind, rid
himself of what had happened in that moment when he'd
stood up and turned to face her. When he'd looked back,
knowing that she'd be there at the window. Wishing he'd
taken her with him when he'd left. When he'd hovered for
a dangerous moment on the point of turning back…

Wouldn't Morgan have loved that?

He stopped drawing and just let his mind's eye see her,
imagining how he'd paint her, sculpt her and when, finally,
he looked up, he'd gone way past his stop.

Tash sat back in the cab as the driver pulled away from the
kerb, did a U-turn and joined the queue of traffic backed
up along the King's Road.

A little more than twenty minutes—just long enough to
get a parking ticket—that was all it had taken to reduce her
from top-selling negotiator at one of the most prestigious
estate agencies in London, to unemployable.

'It's a beautiful house, Darius.' Patsy, having dropped off
some paperwork and made them both a cup of tea, had
discovered the *Chronicle* in the waste bin when she'd dis-
carded the teabags. 'Lots of room. You could make a studio in one of the buildings,' she said with a head jerk that
took in the concrete walls and floor still stained with oil

from its previous incarnation as a motor repair shop. 'Why don't you just move in? Ask me nicely and I might even come and keep house for you.'

'You and whose army?' He glanced at the photograph of the sprawling house, its Tudor core having been added to over the centuries by ancestors with varying degrees of taste. At least someone had done their job right, taking time to find the perfect spot to show the Chase at its best. The half-timbering, a mass of roses hiding a multitude of sins. A little to the right of a cedar tree that had been planted to commemorate the coronation of Queen Victoria.

The perfect spot at the perfect time on the perfect day when a golden mist rising from the river had lent the place an ethereal quality that took him back to school holidays and early-morning fishing trips with his grandfather. Took him back to an enchanted world seen through the innocent eyes of a child.

'It's got at least twenty rooms,' he said, returning to the armature on which he was building his interpretation of a racehorse flying over a fence. 'That's not including the kitchen, scullery, pantries and the freezing attics where the poor sods who kept the place running in the old days were housed.' Plus half a dozen cottages, at present occupied by former employees of the estate whom he could never evict, and a boat house that was well past its best twenty years ago.

She put the magazine on his workbench where he could see it, opened a packet of biscuits and, when he shook his head, helped herself to one. 'So what are you going to do?'

'Wring that wretched girl's neck?' he offered, and tried not to think about his hand curled around her nape. How her skin would feel against his palm, the scent of vanilla that he couldn't lose… 'Subject closed.'

He picked up the *Chronicle* and tossed it back in the bin.

'It said in the paper that she'd had some kind of a break-down,' Patsy protested.

A widow, she worked as a freelance 'Girl Friday' for several local businesses, fitting them in around the needs of her ten-year-old son. She kept his books and his paper-work in order, the fridge stocked with fresh milk, cold beer, and his life organised. The downside was that, like an old time travelling minstrel, she delivered neighbour-hood gossip, adding to the story with each stop she made. He had no doubt that Hadley Chase had featured heavily in her story arc this week and her audience were no doubt eagerly awaiting the next instalment.

'Please tell me you don't believe everything you read in the newspapers,' he said as, concentration gone, he gave up on the horse and drank the tea he hadn't asked for.

'Of course I don't,' she declared, 'but the implication was that she had a history of instability. They wouldn't lie about something like that.' She took another biscuit, clearly in no hurry to be anywhere else.

'No? She was in full control of her faculties when I saw her,' he said. 'I suspect the breakdown story is Morgan and Black's attempt to focus the blame on her and lessen the impact on their business.' Lessen the damages.

'That's shocking. She should sue.'

'She hasn't bothered to deny it,' he said.

'Maybe her lawyer has advised her not to say anything. What's she like? You didn't say you'd met her.'

'Believe me,' he said, 'I'm doing my best to forget.' For-get his body's slamming response at the sight of her. The siren call of a sensually pleasing body that had been made to wrap around a man. A mouth made for pleasure. The feeling of control slipping away from him.

Precious little chance of that when his hands itched to capture the liquid blue of eyes that had sucked the breath out of him, sent the blood rushing south, nailing him to the spot. A look that eluded his every attempt to recreate it.

It was just as well she was safely out of reach in the Fairview, playing along with Morgan's game in the hopes of hanging on to her job. Asking her to sit for him was a distraction he could not afford. And would certainly not endear him to his lawyers.

'I wonder if it was anorexia?' she pondered. 'In the past.' Patsy, generous in both character and build, took another biscuit.

'No way.' He shook his head as he recalled that delicious moment when, as Natasha Gordon had offered him her hand, the top button of her blouse had surrendered to the strain, parting to reveal the kind of cleavage any red-blooded male would willingly dive into. 'Natasha Gordon has all the abundant charms of a milkmaid.'

'A milkmaid?'

Patsy's grandparents had immigrated to Britain in the nineteen-fifties and she'd lived her entire life in the inner city. It was likely that the closest she'd ever come to a cow was in a children's picture book.

'Big blue eyes, a mass of fair hair and skin like an old-fashioned rose.' There was one that scrambled over the rear courtyard at the Chase. He had no idea what it was called, but it had creamy petals blushed with pink that were bursting out of a calyx not designed to contain such bounty. 'Believe me, this is not a woman who lives on lettuce.'

'Oh…' She gave him an old-fashioned look. 'And did this milkmaid apologise with a pretty curtsy?' she asked, confirming her familiarity with the genre.

'She didn't appear to have read the script.' No apology, no excuses… 'She suggested that the advertisement was little more than a minor setback.'

'Really? You're quite sure the poor woman is not cracking up?'

'As sure as I can be without a doctor's note.' But there was a distinct possibility that he was.

Milkmaids, roses…

Forget wheeling her in to apologise. If it was possible to be any more cynical, he'd have said they were hoping that she might use her charms, her lack of control over her buttons, to distract him from taking legal action.

He shouldn't even be thinking about how far she might go to achieve that objective. Or how happy he would be to lie back and let her try.

'Dad's really worried about you, Tash. You've been working so hard and all this stress…well…you know…' Her mother never actually said what she was thinking out loud. 'He thinks you should come home for a while so that we can look after you.'

Tash sighed. She'd known that whatever she said, they'd half believe the newspaper story, convinced that they had been right all along. That she would be safer at home. No matter how much she told herself that they were wrong, it was hard to resist that kind of worry.

'Mum, I'm fine.'

'Tom thinks a break would do you good. We've booked the house down in Cornwall for the half-term holiday.' So far, so what she'd expected. Her dad the worrier, her brother the doctor prescribing a week at the seaside and her mother trying to please everyone. 'You know how you always loved it there and you haven't seen the children for ages. You won't believe how they've grown.'

Twenty-five and on holiday with her family. Building sandcastles for her nieces during the day and playing Scrabble or Monopoly in the evening. How appealing was that?

'I saw them at Easter,' she said. 'Send me a postcard.'

'Darling…'

'It's all smoke and mirrors, Mum. I'm fit as a flea.'

'Are you sure? Are you taking the vitamins I sent you?'

'I never miss,' she said, rolling her eyes in exasperation. She understood, really, but anyone would think she was still five years old and fighting for her life instead of a successful career woman. This was just a hiccup.

'Are you eating properly?'

'All the food groups.'

When the taxi had delivered her to her door, she'd gone straight to the freezer and dug out a tub of strawberry cheesecake ice cream. While she'd eaten it, she pulled up the file on her laptop so that if, in a worst case scenario, it came to an unfair dismissal tribunal she had a paper trail to demonstrate exactly what she'd done. Except that there it all was, word for word, on the screen. Exactly as printed. Which made no sense.

The proof copy she'd seen, approved and put in her out tray had been the one she'd actually written, not the one that was printed.

Either she really was going mad or someone had gone out of their way to do this to her. Not just changing the original copy, fiddling with the proof and intercepting the phone call from the *Chronicle*, but getting into her laptop to change what she'd written so that she had no proof that she'd ever written anything else.

Okay, a forensic search would pull up the original, but there would be no way to prove that she hadn't changed it herself because whoever had done this had logged in using her password.

Which meant there was only one person in the frame.

The man who hadn't let her know he was back a week early from a six-week rugby tour. The man who hadn't come rushing round with pizza, Chianti and chocolate the minute he heard the news. Who hadn't called, texted, emailed even, to ask how she was.

The man who was now occupying the upstairs office that should, by rights, be hers.

Her colleague with benefits: Toby Denton.

She wouldn't have thought the six-foot-three blond rugby-playing hunk—who'd never made a secret of the fact that he saw work as a tedious interruption to his life and whose only ambition was to play the sport professionally—had the brains to engineer her downfall with such cunning.

His cluelessness, off the rugby field, had been a major part of his appeal. When there was any rescuing to be done—which was often when it came to work—she was the one tossing him the lifebelt. Like giving him her laptop password so that he could check the office diary for an early-morning appointment when, typically, he'd forgotten where he was supposed to be.

The announcement of his appointment as associate partner had appeared on the company website the day after she'd been walked to the door with her belongings in a cardboard box. Photographs of the champagne celebration had appeared on the blog a day later. It was great PR and she'd have applauded if it hadn't been her career they were interring.

'Tash?' her mother asked anxiously. 'Are you baking?'

'Baking? No...' Then, in sheer desperation, 'Got to go. Call waiting. Have a lovely time in Cornwall.'

Call waiting... She wished, she thought, glancing along the work surface at the ginger, lemon drizzle and passion cakes lined up alongside a Sacher Torte, waiting for the ganache she was making.

She *had* been baking. She'd used every bowl she possessed, every cake tin. They were piled up in the sink and on the draining board, along with a heap of eggshells and empty sugar, flour and butter wrappers and a fine haze of icing sugar hung in the air, coating every surface, including her.

It was her displacement activity. Some people played endless computer games, or went for a run, or ironed when they needed to let their brain freewheel. She beat butter and sugar and eggs into creamy peaks.

Unfortunately, her mind was ignoring the no-job, no-career problem. Instead it kept running Darius Hadley on a loop. That moment when he'd turned and looked at her in Miles Morgan's office, his face all dark shadows, his eyes burning into her. His hands. The glint of gold beneath dark curls. The air stirring as he'd walked past her, leaving the scent of something earthy behind.

That moment when he'd stopped in the street and looked back and she'd known that if he'd lifted a hand to her she would have gone to him. Worse, had wanted him to lift a hand...

Her skin glowed just thinking about that look. Not just her skin.

Madness.

Her skin was sticky, her eyes gritty; she had no job and no one was going to call. Not Miles. Not any of the agencies that had tried to tempt her away from him. Last week she was the negotiator everyone wanted on their team, but now she was damaged goods.

If she was going to rescue her career, this was going to have to be a show rather than tell scenario. She would have to demonstrate to the world that she was still the best there was. Her brain hadn't been dodging the problem; it had been showing her the answer.

Darius Hadley.

She was going to have to find a buyer for Hadley Chase.

A week ago that had been a challenge, but she'd had the contacts, people who would pick up the phone when she called, listen to her when she told them she had exactly the house they were looking for because she didn't lie, didn't waste their time. Matching houses with the right buyers was a passion with her. People trusted her. Or they had.

Now the word on the street was that she'd lost it. She was on her own with nothing to offer except her wits, her knowledge of the market and the kind of motivation that would move mountains if she could persuade Darius Hadley to give her a chance.

She was going to have to face him: this man who'd turned her into a blushing, jelly-boned cliché with no more than a look.

In the normal course of events it wouldn't have been more than a momentary wobble. It had been made clear to her by the estate's executor that the vendor wanted nothing to do with the actual sale of his house and if he'd let her just get on with it she would never have seen him again. Apparently her luck had hit the deck on all fronts that morning.

At the time she hadn't given the reason why Darius Hadley was keeping his distance any thought—it had taken all her concentration not to melt into a puddle at his feet—but the more she'd thought about him, the more she understood how it must hurt to be the Hadley to let the house go. To lose four centuries of his family history.

If there was no cash to go with the property, he would have no choice—death meant taxes—but it was easy to see why he'd been furious with them, with *her*, for messing up and forcing him to confront the situation head-on. Maybe, though, now he'd had time to calm down, he'd be glad of someone offering to help.

Selling a country estate was an expensive business. Printing, advertising, travel, and she doubted that, in these cash-strapped days, he'd be inundated with estate agents eager to invest in a house that had been publicly declared a money pit.

Hopefully she'd be all he'd got. And he, collywobbles notwithstanding, was almost certainly her only hope.

Fortunately she had all the details of Hadley Chase on her laptop.

What she didn't have were the contact details for Darius Hadley.

She'd had no success when she'd searched Hadley Chase on Google hoping for some family gossip to get the property page editors salivating. She assumed it would have thrown up anything newsworthy about Darius Hadley, but she typed his name into the search engine anyway.

A whole load of links came up, including images, and she clicked on the only one of him. It had been taken, ironically, from one of those high society functions featured in the *Country Chronicle* and the caption read: 'Award-winning sculptor Darius Hadley at the Serpentine Gallery...'

He was a sculptor? Well, that would explain the steel toecaps, the grey smears on his jeans. That earthy scent had been clay...

His tie was loose, his collar open and he'd been caught unawares, laughing at something or someone out of the picture and she was right. A smile was all it took to lift the shadows. He still had the look of the devil, but one who was having a good day, and she reached out and touched the screen, her fingertips against his mouth.

'Oh...' she breathed. 'Collywollydoodah...'

CHAPTER THREE

THE NARROW COBBLED backstreet was a jumble of buildings that had been endlessly converted and added to over the centuries. All Tash had was the street name, but she had been confident that a prize-winning sculptor's studio would be easy enough to find.

She was wrong.

She'd reached a dead end and found no sign, no indication that art of any kind happened behind any of the doors but as she turned she found herself face-to-face with a woman who was regarding her through narrowed eyes.

'Can I help you?' she asked.

'I hope so… I'm looking for Darius Hadley. I was told his studio was in this street,' she prompted.

The woman gave her a long, thoughtful look, taking in the grey business suit that she kept for meetings with the property managers of billionaires; she had hoped it would cut down on the inexplicable electricity that had sparked between them in Miles's office. A spark that had sizzled even when he was outside on the pavement looking up at her.

Okay, maybe she should have worn a pair of sensible, low-heeled shoes, added horn-rimmed spectacles to make herself look *seriously* serious. Hell, she *was* serious, never more so—this was her career on the line—but there was only so far she could stretch the illusion. As for her favourite red heels, she'd needed them to give her a little extra

height, some of the bounce that had been knocked clean
out of her. Besides, Darius Hadley wouldn't be fooled by
a pair of faux specs. Not for a minute.

She'd experienced the power of eyes that would see right
through any games, any pretence and knew that she would
have to be absolutely straight with him.

No problem. Straight was what she did and she had it
all worked out. The look, the poise, what she was going to
say. She was going to be totally professional, which was
all very fine in theory but first she had to find him. She'd
called in a big favour to get his address but now she was
beginning to wonder if she'd been sold a fake.

The woman, her inspection completed, asked, 'Is Darius expecting you?'

'He'll want to see me,' she said, fingers mentally crossed.
'Do you know him?'

'Sure,' she said, a slow smile lighting up her face. 'I
know everyone. Even you, Natasha Gordon.'

Tash, still dragging her chin back into place, followed
the woman back down the street towards a pair of wide,
rusty old garage doors over which a sign suggested someone called Mike would repair your car while you waited.
She produced a large bunch of keys and let herself in
through the personnel door.

'Darius?' she called, leaving the door open. Tash, grabbing her chance, stepped in after her. 'How are you feeling
about the milkmaid today?'

Milkmaid?

There was a discouraging grunt from somewhere above
her head. 'Not now, Patsy.'

She looked up. Darius Hadley was standing on a tall
stepladder, thumbing clay onto the leaping figure of a horse.

'Do you still want to wring her neck?' Patsy persisted.

'Nothing has changed since last week,' he replied, leaning back a little to check what he'd done, 'but, to put your

mind at rest, that damned house has given me enough trouble without adding grievous bodily harm to the list.'

'So it would be safe to let her in?'

Now she had his attention.

'Let her...' He swung around and her heart leapt. He was so high... 'She's *here*?'

'She doesn't have a milking stool, or one of those things they wear across the shoulders with a pail at each end, but other than that she fits the description. Abundantly,' she added with a broad smile. 'Of course it helped that you've been drawing her on any bit of paper that comes to hand for the last few days.'

'Patsy...'

'I found her wandering up and down the street looking for your studio. Your name on the door would be a real help,' she said, apparently not the least bit intimidated by the growl.

'That would only encourage visitors. People who interrupt me while I'm working,' he said, looking over Patsy's head to where she was hovering just inside the doorway.

Maybe it was just the sunlight streaming in through the skylight above him, but today his eyes were molten slate, scorching her skin, melting the starch in her shirt, reducing her knees to fudge frosting.

It wasn't just his eyes. Everything about him was hot: the faded, clay-smeared jeans hugging his thighs, midnight-black hair curling into his neck, long, ropey muscles in his forearms. And those hands...

She had tried to convince herself that she'd imagined the electricity, the fizz, the crackle... There had been a shock factor when she'd seen him in Miles's office, but he'd been in her head for days and not just because he was her only chance to get back to work.

She'd been dreaming about those hands. How they'd feel on her body, the drag of hard calluses against tender skin...

'I know I'm the last person on earth you want to talk to, Mr Hadley,' she said quickly before he could tell her to get lost, 'but if you can spare me ten minutes, I've got a proposition for you.'

'Proposition?'

The word hung in the air.

Darius looked down at the shadowy hourglass shape of Natasha Gordon, backlit by sunlight streaming in over the city rooftops.

It was just a word. Morgan couldn't possibly be using her as a sweetener. But then again, maybe it was her idea...

'If you could spare me ten minutes?' From above her he could see straight down the opening of her blouse, the way her luscious breasts were squished together as she raised her hand to shield her eyes from the light pouring in from the skylights. 'Maybe we could sit down,' she suggested, lifting her other hand a little to show him a glossy white cakebox, dangling from a ribbon. 'I've brought cake. It's home-made. I'll even make the tea.'

He picked up a damp cloth and wiped his hands, giving himself a moment to still his rampaging libido. He should send her packing but how often did a man receive a proposition from a sexy woman bearing cake? And now she was here he'd be able to capture the look that had eluded him, draw her out of his head.

'I hope you or your mother can cook,' he said and Patsy nodded, apparently satisfied that it would be safe to leave him alone with her, and left them to it.

'Would I come bearing anything less than perfection?' she asked.

Not this woman, he thought. She'd pulled out all the stops... 'How did you find me?'

'Does it matter?' she asked, the wide space between her brows crumpled in a tiny frown that didn't fool him for a moment. Not many people knew where he worked. She'd had to work hard to locate him.

'Humour me,' he suggested, taking a step down the ladder, and she caught her breath, muscles tensed, barely stopping herself from taking a step back. She was nowhere near as cool as she looked. Which made two of them.

'I did what anyone would do. Ran an Internet search,' she said quickly, 'and there you were. Darius Hadley, award-winning sculptor, presently working on a prestigious commission to create a life-size bronze of one of the greatest racehorses of all time.' Lots of details so he'd forget the question. He was familiar with the technique. His grandfather had been a past master at diverting him whenever he'd asked awkward questions. 'There was a photograph,' she added.

'Of me?' He took another step down. She swallowed, but this time stood her ground.

'Of the horse. It was in the *Racing Times*. Photographs of you are scarce. You don't even have a website.' She made it sound like an accusation.

'I seem to manage.'

'Yes…'

She turned away, giving them both a break as she looked around at the dozens of photographs taken from every angle of the horse—galloping, jumping, standing—that he'd pinned to the walls. She paused briefly at the anatomical drawings of the skeleton, the muscles, the blood vessels and then looked up at his interpretation of the animal gathered to leap a jump.

'If I'd known who you were when the house came on the market,' she said at last, 'I could have used the information to get some editorial interest. Racehorse owners are among the richest men in the world and Hadley Chase is close to one of the country's major racehorse training centres.'

'You managed an excessive number of column inches

without any help from me,' he said, 'but that's who, not
where,' he said, refusing to be sidetracked.

A rueful smile made it to a mouth that was a little too big
for beauty, tugging it upwards. 'The where *was* more difficult. And the address was only half the story. If it hadn't
been for Patsy I'd still be looking for you.'

'So?' he insisted.

'I'm sorry, Mr Hadley. An estate agent never reveals
her sources.'

'A journalist?' No, the piece in the newspaper had not
been kind. Reading between the lines, anyone would be
forgiven for assuming her 'collapse' had been the result of
a coke-fuelled drive for success. Something in her past...
Journalists would not be flavour of the month. 'An art
dealer?' he suggested. Who would be vulnerable to those
big blue eyes and a loose top button? No... Who had moved
recently? 'Freddie Glover threw a house-warming party a
few months back,' he said.

She neither confirmed nor denied it and, satisfied, he
let it rest.

'If you've come to apologise...' She seemed bright
enough so he left her to fill in the blank.

'I was sure Miles would have performed the ritual grovel
but I could go through the motions if you insist,' she offered.

A little movement of her hand, underlining the offer,
sent a barely discernible shimmer through her body—a
shimmer that found an answering echo deep in his groin.
Yes...

She waited briefly, but he was too busy catching his
own breath to answer.

'I'm sorry about what happened, obviously, but that's
not the reason I'm here.'

'Why are you here?' he demanded. He hated being
this out of control around a woman. Could not make him-

self send her away. 'For heaven's sake, come in and close the door if you're staying. I won't eat you...'

She didn't look entirely convinced, but she closed the door, took a breath and then walked towards him with the kind of mesmerisingly slow, hip-swaying walk that had gone out of style fifty years ago. Around the same time as her hourglass figure.

No longer backlit from the street, the light pouring in from the skylights overhead lit her up like a spotlight and he could see that she'd made an attempt to disguise its lushness beneath a neat grey suit. Or maybe not. The skirt clung to her thighs and stopped a hand's breadth short of serious, leaving a yard of leg on display, always supposing he'd got past the deep vee of her shirt. She really should try a size larger if she was serious.

As for her hair, she'd fastened it in a sleek twist that rested against the nape of her neck; it was a classically provocative style and his fingers, severely provoked, itched to pull the pins and send it tumbling around her face and shoulders.

She'd stopped a teasing arm's width from the ladder, looking up at him. Near enough for the honeyed scent of warm skin, something lemony, spicy, chocolatey to reach him but, maybe sensing the danger, not quite close enough to touch. Clearly her instincts were better honed than his because every beat of his pulse urged him to reach for her, pull her close enough to feel what she was doing to him...

Forget the cake. Eating her, one luscious mouthful at a time, was the only thing on his mind.

'Well?' he snapped. Angry with her for disturbing him. No one was allowed to disturb him while he was working. Angry with himself for wanting to be disturbed. For the triumphant *Yes!* racketing through him at her unexpected appearance, despite the certainty that this was some devi-

ous scheme of Morgan's—sending in the sex bomb to persuade him to drop his claim for damages.

Tash ran her tongue over her teeth in an attempt to get
some spit so that she could answer him. Lay out her offer
like the professional she was.

She was used to meeting powerful men and women but
she was having a tough job remembering why she was in
Darius Hadley's studio. The concrete floor and walls made
the space cold after the sun outside, but a trickle of sweat
was running down between her breasts and an age-old instinct was telling her to shrug off her jacket, let her hair
down, reach out and run her fingers up his denim-clad
thigh, perched, tantalisingly, at eye level.

'What do you want, Natasha Gordon?'

She looked up and saw her feelings echoed in Darius
Hadley's shadowed features and for a moment it could have
gone either way.

She was saved by the crash of a pigeon landing on the
skylight, startling them both out of the danger zone.

'I don't want anything from you, Mr Hadley,' she said
quickly. Could this be any more difficult? Bad enough that
he thought she'd sabotaged the sale of his house without
acting like a sex-starved nymphomaniac. 'On the contrary.
I'm going to do you a favour. I'm going to sell your house
for you.'

'Miss Gordon…'

'I know.' She held up her hand in a gesture of surren-
der. 'Why would you trust me? After the debacle with your
ad,' she added, and then wished she hadn't. Having found
him, got through the door a darn sight more easily than
she'd expected and survived that first intense encounter,
reminding him why he should throw her out was not her
brightest move.

'Is there any hope that you're not going to tell me?'
he asked.

Phew… 'Not a chance.' She slipped the strap of her laptop bag from her shoulder and let it drop at her feet, anchoring herself in his space. Then she placed the glossy white cakebox on his workbench alongside his neatly laid-out tools—most of which appeared to be lethal weapons. Most, but not all. She picked up a long curved rib bone.

'That belonged to the last person who annoyed me,' he said, finally stepping off the ladder.

'Really?' Apparently there was a sense of humour lurking beneath that scowl. Promising…

'What did he do?' she asked, looking up at the sculpture rearing above her, heart swelling within its ribcage as the horse leapt some unseen obstacle. From what she'd seen of his work on the Net, it appeared that visceral was something of a theme. 'Did he throw you? Is this you getting your own back?'

'Anyone can make a pretty image.' He took the bone from her, replaced it on the bench. 'I want to show what's behind the power, the movement. Bones, sinews, heart.'

'The engine rather than the chassis.' Eager to avoid close eye contact, she walked around the beast, examining it from every angle, before looking across at Darius Hadley from the safety of the far side. 'That's what you do, isn't it? Show us the inside of things.'

'That's what's real, what's important.'

'I saw your installation outside Tate Modern. The house.' That had been stripped back to the bones, too.

'You've done your homework,' he said.

'I was just walking past. I didn't realise it was yours until I looked you up online. I thought it was…bleak.'

'Everyone's a critic.'

'No… It was beautiful. It's just…well, there were no people and without them a house is simply a frame.'

'Perhaps that was the point,' he suggested.

'Was it?' He didn't answer and she looked back up at the horse. 'This is…big.'

'I'll cast a smaller version for a limited edition.'

'Just the thing for the mantelpiece,' she said flippantly. Then wished she hadn't. His work was more important than that. 'I'm sorry; that was a stupid thing to say. I'm a bit nervous.'

'I'm not surprised. Does Miles Morgan really think he can buy me off with a glimpse of your cleavage and a slice of cake?'

'What?' She checked her top button but it was still in place. Just. She'd worn her roomiest shirt but working ten, fourteen hours a day didn't leave much time for exercise, or a carefully thought-out diet. And she'd moved less and eaten more in the last week than was good for anyone; it was definitely time to get out of the kitchen and back to work. 'Miles didn't send me. As for the cleavage…' She lifted her shoulders in a little shrug that she hoped would give the impression that she was utterly relaxed. She was good at that. The most important thing she'd learned about selling houses was to create an image. Set the stage, create an initial impact that would grab the viewer's attention then hold it. This time she was selling herself… 'I've been on a baking binge and eating too much of my own cooking.'

'And now you want to share.'

'I thought something sweet might help to break the ice.' Ice?

There was no ice as she bent forward to tug on the gauzy bow that exactly matched the shade of her lipstick, her nails; only heat zinging through his veins, making the blood pump thickly in his ears.

He'd been drawing her obsessively for a week, trying to get her out of his head, but while the two-dimensional image had been recognisable it lacked the warmth, the sparkle of the original.

Right now all he wanted to do was peel away her clothes, expose those rich creamy curves to the play of sunlight and shade.

He wanted to draw her from every angle, stripping away layer after layer until he could see her core. Until he could see what she was thinking, what she was feeling; transmute that into a three-dimensional image exposing the heart of the woman within.

He wanted a lot more than that.

'What have you got?' he asked.

'I wasn't sure which you'd like so I brought a selection,' she said, looking at him. For a moment the air seemed to crackle and then she was looking down at the box, her eyes hidden by silky lashes. 'There's lemon drizzle, chocolate, coffee, sticky ginger and, um, passion cake.'

The scent of vanilla rose enticingly from the box, taking him straight back to his childhood—that sweet moment when he'd been allowed to lick the remains of the mixture from the spoon; when he'd sunk his teeth into a cake still warm from the oven.

He was no longer a boy but he resisted one temptation only to look up and find himself confronted by the reach-out-and-touch-me lure of warm breasts.

Was this how it had been for his father? An obsessive urge to possess one woman wiping everything from his mind. One woman becoming his entire world.

Stick to the cake...

'You weren't kidding when you said you'd been on a baking binge, Miss Gordon,' he said, taking the first piece his fingers touched, anything to distract him. 'Did the Fairview recommend it as occupational therapy?'

'Tash, please. Everyone calls me Tash.'

'I prefer Natasha,' he said, sucking the icing from his thumb, and she blushed. Not the swift suffusion of heat that rose to her face in that moment when they'd confronted one another in Morgan's office and seen how it would be if they ever let their guard down, but a real girlish blush.

'Nobody calls me that,' she said. 'Only my mother. When I've done something to exasperate her.'

'That would be your mother and me, then.'

'Point taken.' The corner of her mouth tilted upwards in a wry sketch at a smile. 'I'd be annoyed with me if I were you. I'm pretty annoyed myself, to be honest. It wasn't much fun having to phone my parents and warn them that they and their neighbours and everyone they knew would be reading about my breakdown in the evening paper. Warn them that they'd probably have reporters ringing them at home, knocking on the door. Which they did, by the way.'

'No comment.'

The smile deepened to reveal a small crease in her cheek. She'd once had a dimple…

'It's not true, by the way. About the Fairview. In case you were in any doubt. Just so that we're on the same page here, Miles Morgan and I parted company less than fifteen minutes after you left the office.'

'He fired you?' He should have waited. Gone back. Followed his gut instinct to grab her hand and take her with him… 'I'm not big on employment law but I'm fairly sure he can't have it both ways. He can't dismiss you when you're on sick leave.'

'You're probably right,' she admitted, 'but I refused to cooperate with his plan to have my sanity publicly questioned and hide away in the Fairview in the cause of saving the firm's reputation.'

'I saw the paper.'

'Everyone saw the paper,' she said. 'I'm supposedly giving my brain a rest in the Fairview while I consider my future.'

'You didn't deny it,' he pointed out.

'Like that would have helped.' She clutched at her throat

with both hands. '*I'm not mad. It wasn't me. I was framed!*' she croaked out, rolling her eyes, feigning madness.

He was expected to laugh, but it was taking all his concentration just to breathe because she'd forgotten not to look at him. And then she remembered and he could see that it wasn't just him. They were both struggling with the zing of lightning that arced between them.

'Since Plan B was a threat to sue me for malicious damage...' Her voice was thick, her pupils huge against the shot-silk blue; what would she do if he reached out and took her hand and held it against his zip, if he sucked her lower lip into his mouth? '...I didn't think there was much point in hanging around.'

He turned away, crossed to the kettle, picking it up to make sure there was some water in it before switching it on. Any distraction from the thoughts racketing through his head. The same thoughts that had driven him from Morgan's office amplified a hundred times.

He had no problem with lust at first sight. Uncomplicated, life's-too-short sex that gave everyone a good time and didn't screw with your head. This was complicated with knobs on. He should never have let her stay.

He could not have sent her away...

'It's a bit like denying Hadley Chase is riddled with woodworm,' he said, tossing teabags into a couple of mugs, making an effort to bring the conversation back to the house—as effective as any cold shower. 'Once it's in print, who's going to believe you?'

'Exactly... Not that it is,' she said, as eager as him to get back to business, apparently. 'Riddled with woodworm. The house has been neglected in recent years, the roof needs some work, but the structure is sound and the advertisement did get people talking about the house,' she stressed earnestly, as if that were something to be welcomed. 'My photograph was reprinted in all the weekend property supplements.'

'Your photograph?' He waved her towards the ancient sofa that he sometimes slept on when he'd worked late and he was too tired to stagger the hundred yards home. 'Didn't Morgan employ a professional?'

'Oh, yes, and he did his best with the interior, but it was raining on the day he was there so, despite his best efforts with Photoshop, his exteriors weren't doing the house any favours,' she said, sinking into the low saggy cushions. 'We were running out of time so, when the weather changed at the weekend, I grabbed the chance to dash down the motorway early on Sunday and take some myself.'

'You've got a good eye.'

'Oh, I took hundreds of pictures. That one just leapt out at me.'

It was more than that, he thought, getting out the milk, keeping his hands busy. She'd taken the trouble to go back in her own time. Given it one hundred per cent… 'It's a pity the property pages didn't just stick to the photograph.'

'That was never going to happen. It was too good a story to pass up on and it was a fabulous PR opportunity. If Miles hadn't panicked…' She paused, as if something was bothering her.

'What? What would you have done?'

'Oh… Well, first I'd have got in a firm of cleaners at the firm's expense. Then I'd have invited the property editors to lunch at the Hadley Arms and, once I'd got them gagging at the perfect picture postcard village, I'd have driven them up to the house, slowly enough so that they could appreciate the view, that first glimpse as the house appears.'

'And then?'

'Well, obviously,' she said, 'I'd have got you an offer within the week.'

Her smile was bright and as brittle as spun sugar. He

wanted the real thing. Not just mouth and teeth, but those eyes lit up, glowing…

'Despite the dodgy staircase and the leaking roof?' he pressed.

She tutted but it earned him a hint of what her smile could be. 'It hasn't rained all week.'

'This hot spell can't last.'

'No, which is why we need to get cracking. Hadley Chase has so much *potential*,' she continued. 'I hadn't re-alised the extent of the outbuildings until I went down by myself. The stables, the dairy and how many houses have got a brewery, for heaven's sake?'

'It was standard for big houses back in the day, when drinking small beer was safer than water. It hasn't been used in my lifetime. Nor has the dairy.'

'Maybe not, but they're ripe for conversion into work-shops, holiday accommodation, offices. Miles isn't usually so slow…' She let it go, a tiny frown buckling the smooth skin between her brows. 'My mistake.'

'Surely it was his?'

'It's a little more complicated than that.'

She propped her elbow on the arm of the sofa, chin on hand, giving him another flash of her assets. By way of distraction, he picked up the cakebox and offered it to her.

'You do still want to sell the house?' she said as she leaned forward and did an eeny-meeny-miny-mo over the cakes with a dark red fingernail before choosing one.

Some distraction.

'I assumed you'd been sent by Morgan to persuade me to drop my suit,' he said, helping himself to another look straight down the front of her shirt. She was wearing one of those lace traffic-accident bras and all the blood in his brain went south.

She looked up when he didn't say any more. 'Do you still think that?'

Thinking? Who was thinking… He shook his head. 'No. You're pitching for the business.'

She looked up, no smile now, just determination. 'This isn't business, it's personal. What you do about Morgan and Black is your own affair, but my expertise won't cost you a penny.' She gave another of those little shrugs and, as she recrossed her legs, he switched from imperial to metric. A metre…

It had to be deliberate, but he didn't care.

'Of course, if you'd rather sit back and wait a year or two for the fuss to die down…?' she offered before biting into a small square of lemon drizzle cake, her teeth sinking into the softness of the sponge. White teeth, rose petal lips…

Forget the inner woman, he wanted to draw her naked, wanted to mould that luscious body in clay, learn the shape with his hands and then recreate it. Wanted to taste the tip of her tongue as it sought out the sugar clinging to her lip…

'You *might* be lucky,' she said, cucumber-cool, apparently unaware of the effect she was having or of the turmoil raging within him. 'It might be a big news week in the property business and they won't dredge up the story all over again. Reprint the original advertisement.' She finished the tiny square of cake, sucked the stickiness off a fingertip. It was deliberate and he discovered that he didn't care. Just as long as she went on doing it. 'I'll leave you to imagine how likely that is.'

'You seem to forget, Natasha, that I've seen your expertise at first hand.'

'What you've seen, Mr Hadley, is me being stitched up by a man who wanted the promotion I'd worked my socks off for without the bother of putting in the hours.' A fine rim of sugar, missed by her tongue, glistened on her upper lip.

'Darius,' he said, aware that a film of sweat had broken

out above his own lip. Whatever it was she was doing, it was working. 'Only my accountant calls me Mr Hadley.'

He expected her to come back with *your accountant and me*. Instead, she said, 'I'm sorry, Darius. When I said it was a bit more complicated than you thought, I meant really *complicated*.' She looked up, her eyes intent and just a touch desperate. 'The mess-up with the advertisement wasn't a mistake.'

'Not a mistake?'

'Not a mistake,' she repeated, 'but *I* was the target. You were just collateral damage.'

CHAPTER FOUR

'COLLATERAL...?' DARIUS REPEATED, rerunning what she'd said through his head. 'Are you saying this was all about some internal power play at Morgan and Black? That it was deliberate?'

'I really am sorry,' she repeated.

'Not half as sorry as I am.' Or Miles Morgan would be if it was true. 'Did he get it? Your promotion?'

A sigh of relief rippled through her. 'My promotion, my car and, as the icing on the cake, my reputation down the drain.'

The desperation had been fear, he realised. She'd been afraid that he would laugh out loud or call her a liar. The truth of the matter was that he didn't know what to think. It seemed preposterous and yet he'd already half convinced himself that she hadn't messed up the ad. Apparently Freddie Glover wasn't the only one susceptible to a pair of blue eyes and a great pair of—

'The kettle seems to have boiled. Shall I make the tea?' she asked.

'You did volunteer.' Tea was the furthest thing from his mind, but it gave them both a moment and, besides, he wanted to watch her move. The lift of her head, the unfolding of her legs, the muscles in a long shapely calf as she fought the clutches of the sofa. 'Why did he want to destroy your reputation?' he asked, reaching on automatic for his sketch pad, a pencil, working swiftly to capture the image. The lines of her neck, her shoulders as she clicked the kettle back on. Her back and legs as she bent to open the fridge. 'Wasn't your promotion enough?'

'There was no other way of being certain I'd be history,' she said, concentrating on opening a carton of milk. 'I'm really good at my job.'

After an initial wobble when she'd looked as if she wanted to tear his clothes off, Natasha Gordon was doing a very good job of presenting herself as a woman totally in control of her emotions but her eyes betrayed her. A pulse was visible at her throat and if he slid his hand inside the open invitation of her shirt, laid his palm against her breast, he knew he would feel her heart pounding with rage.

The pencil he was holding snapped...

'So are you looking for revenge?' he asked.

'I have my revenge,' she said, losing patience with the carton and jabbing the end of a spoon into the seal as if stabbing whoever had done this to her through the heart. Milk shot over the sleeve of her jacket and, embarrassed, she laughed. 'Okay, maybe I do have issues, but Miles Morgan was panicked into grabbing the first answer that presented itself. No doubt with a little prompting from...' Catching herself, she slipped off the jacket and used a piece of kitchen paper to mop the milk from her sleeve.

'From?'

Right at that moment he didn't much care about the who or the why, he simply wanted to keep her looking like that, and the stub of his pencil continued to work as she shook her head and a wisp of hair escaped the prim little knot, floating for a moment before settling against her cheek.

She frowned. 'I can't be sure. It all happened so fast... Someone had it all worked out in advance and knew exactly which buttons to press.' She pulled a face. 'There's nothing like a champagne celebration to show the world that it's business as usual.'

'Does this someone have a name? I'm sure my lawyer would like to know.'

'No doubt, but I'm not here to help you bring them down,' she said. Nevertheless, the tiny frown persisted. She wanted answers, too.

'So you do want your job back,' he pushed.

'That's not going to happen.'

'You won't work for the man who took your job?'

She shrugged, managed a smile of sorts. 'Never say never. Who knows how desperate I'll get…? How do you like your tea?' she asked, glancing across at him. 'Weak, medium, stand up your spoon…' She stopped. 'Are you drawing me?'

'Yes. Do you mind?'

'I'm not sure.'

'I'll stop if you insist,' he said. 'And strong. Dash of milk. No sugar. You think Morgan will regret it?' he asked, dragging his gaze from his contemplation of her long upper lip just long enough to commit it to paper. 'Grabbing the easy option?'

'Who knows? Toby's bright enough, but he's never allowed work to interfere with his weekends on the rugby field. He's always put that first. To be honest, I never thought he was that interested in property sales and management. I had the impression that his family had pushed him into the day job.'

Toby. He logged the name to look up later. 'I'm surprised he got the job at all if that's his attitude.'

'His great-aunt is married to Peter Black.'

'Oh.'

'He's just turned twenty-three,' she said thoughtfully. 'Maybe he's realised he's not going to get a professional contract.'

'He lost his dream so stole yours? It demonstrates a ruth-less streak. That's vital in business, or so I'm told.'

'It's a trait he kept well hidden. I still find it hard to be-lieve...' She shrugged, letting whatever it was she found hard to believe go. 'Lazy and ruthless is a bad combi-nation, Darius. Would you want him at your back in a crisis? More to the point, would you want to work for a man who'd thrown you to the wolves without a proper hearing? Without any kind of investigation? Forget Toby Denton. He might have my promotion, but it'll always be second best as far as he's concerned. It's Miles I can't forgive. It'll be a cold day in hell before I work for him again.'

'Never say never,' he reminded her and got a reprise of the smile for his pains.

'Maybe if he offered me a full partnership,' she said, 'which is undoubtedly his version of a cold day in hell at the moment.'

'Okay, I get it. It's not going to happen, but if you don't want revenge,' he asked, 'and you don't want your job back, what do you want?'

Natasha's shoulders dropped a fraction. Darius knew that he'd asked the right question, but didn't know whether to kick himself or cheer as her lips softened into the smile he'd asked for. The one that reached her eyes.

His body was divided on the issue; his brain was defi-nitely up for the kicking while the rest of him was respond-ing like a Labrador puppy offered a biscuit.

While he distracted himself by capturing her mouth on paper, Natasha cupped her hands around her warm mug, leaned her hip against the arm of the sofa, making herself at home.

'A week ago I could have walked into any real estate agency in London and been offered a job,' she said. 'Since I've become available, my phone has remained ominously silent.'

'Are you surprised?'

'No, and I haven't embarrassed anyone by reminding them of their generous offers.'

'I'm sure they're all extremely grateful for your tact,' he said, unable to resist a smile of his own. Forget the allure of a body made for sin, he was beginning to like Natasha Gordon. She'd just had the feet knocked out from under her but she'd come up fighting.

'I don't imagine they've given me a second thought. I'm history, Darius. I'll have to restore my hard-earned reputation before anyone will give me the time of day.' She paused, evidently hoping he'd chip in at this point. He drew the line of her jaw. Firm, determined... 'The only way I can do that is by selling Hadley Chase,' she said, offering him the opportunity to help her out.

'Then you really are in trouble.'

'That makes two of us,' she said, taking a sip of her tea. 'I admit that it will require a certain amount of ingenuity and imagination to pull it off, but who has a bigger incentive?' She looked sideways at him, blinking as she caught him staring at her, but this time she didn't look away. 'Who would work harder to find you a buyer?' she asked. 'And for nothing?' she added as a final incentive.

'For nothing? You'll be drummed out of the estate agents guild,' he warned.

Her lips twitched into another of those little smiles. Parts of him twitched involuntarily in response. His head didn't have a chance.

'Believe me, it's a once-in-a-lifetime offer. What have you got to lose?' Energy, excitement at the challenge poured off her in an almost physical wave. 'We're a match made in heaven.'

He shook his head, afraid that he'd already lost it. He shouldn't even be having the conversation. The lawyers would have a fit.

'An estate agent no one will employ and a house no one can sell? That sounds more like hell to me,' he said, but he was unable to stop himself from laughing. She was bright, intelligent and, under other circumstances—the uncompli-cated, no strings, hot sex circumstances—would no doubt be a lot of fun. Unfortunately, this was getting more com-plicated by the moment.

'I'm not promising heaven,' she protested, 'but it won't be hell. Honestly.'

That he could believe... 'I bet you say that to all the poor saps trying to sell a house in a recession.'

'I do my best to give it to them straight,' she replied. 'And I do everything I can to help them to make the best of the property they're selling. That's my job.'

'Paint it magnolia and hide the clutter in the cupboards?' he suggested.

'Getting rid of the clutter so that you can open the cup-boards is better. Storage space is a big selling point.' She looked at him over the mug. 'Giving the place a good clean helps. Brushing out the dead leaves. Fixing broken win-dows.'

He frowned. 'Are you telling me that there's a broken window at the Chase?'

'You didn't know? I did point it out to your caretaker. He said he'd mention it to the executors.'

And they hadn't bothered to mention it to him. Well, he'd made his position clear enough. Not interested...

'Look, I'm not pretending that it's going to be easy,' she said. 'You're not selling a well-kept four-bed detached house in an area with good schools.'

'I wouldn't need you if I was.'

It was an admission that he did need her and they both knew it.

'What I'm promising, Darius, is that you won't have to be personally involved in any way.' She reached out a sympathetic hand, but curled her fingers back before it touched his arm. Even so, his skin tightened at the imperceptible movement of air and the shiver of it went right through him. 'I do understand how difficult this must be for you.'

'I doubt it.' Nobody could ever begin to understand how he felt about the Chase. The complex mix of memories, emotions it evoked.

'No, of course not, but Hadley Chase has been in your family for centuries. I can see how it must hurt to be the one who has to let it go.'

'Is that what you think?' he asked, looking up from those curled-up fingers, challenging her. 'That I'm ashamed because I've failed to hold on to it?'

'No! Of course not.' The blush flooded back to her cheeks. 'Why should you be? This is the fault of preceding generations.' The possibility that by criticising his recent ancestors she might be digging an even bigger hole for herself must have crossed her mind and she moved swiftly on. 'I'll do everything possible to make this as painless as possible,' she promised. 'All you have to do is let the caretaker and your lawyer know that I'll be handling things on your behalf, then you needn't give it another thought.'

This time his laugh was forced, painful. 'If you could guarantee that you'd have a deal.'

'I can guarantee that I won't disturb you again without a very good reason,' she assured him.

Too late. Natasha Gordon was the most disturbing woman he'd ever met, but the Chase was a millstone around his neck, a darkness at the heart of his family, his grandfather's last-ditch attempt to regain control of a world he'd once dominated, ruled. To control the future. To control him. The sooner he was rid of it, the burden lifted, the better.

'Suppose I agree to let you loose on it,' he said, as if it wasn't already a done deal, 'do you have a plan?'

'A plan?'

'You don't have an advertising budget,' he pointed out, 'or a shop window for passers-by to browse in, or even a listing in the *Yellow Pages*.'

'No, but I do have the Internet, social media.'

Oh, shit…

'Did you say something?'

Not out loud, he was almost certain, but his reaction had been so strong that she had undoubtedly read his mind. 'You can't use my name,' he warned, gesturing around the studio, 'or any of this to generate publicity.' This was his world. He had created it. No one else. He wouldn't have it touched by his family or the Chase.

'It'll be a low-key approach,' she assured him, far too easily. 'Nothing flashy, nothing to embarrass you. You have my word.'

'Your word, in this instance, is worthless. Once it's on the Net you'll lose control.'

'Only if I get it right.'

'Is that supposed to reassure me?'

She frowned, obviously confused by his attitude. 'It's just a house, Darius.'

She was wrong, but he couldn't expect her to understand his love/hate relationship with the place. With his family. 'You've got all the answers,' he said dismissively.

She shook her head. 'If I had all the answers, I wouldn't be here,' she said, 'I'd be at Morgan and Black, lining up viewings with the property managers of the kind of men and women who can afford to buy and maintain an English country house to use for two or three weeks in the year. During the shooting season,' she added, in case he didn't get the point, 'or maybe for Christmas and the New Year, before they move on to Gstaad or Aspen for the skiing.'

'That's…'

'Yes?'

'Nothing.'

He shouldn't care who bought it, or how little they used it… He didn't. And he had no reason to trust her, or to believe that she'd lost her job for anything other than sheer incompetence. Only the fact that Miles Morgan had lied about a breakdown, publicly humiliating her in a way that even if she had been grossly negligent would still have been unforgivable. And that he'd disliked the man on sight.

What Natasha Gordon had done to him on sight was something else. The fact that he wasn't thinking with his brain was reason enough to stay well clear of any harebrained idea she came up with, but the Revenue would not wait forever for the inheritance tax he would have to pay on the estate. The truth of the matter was that he couldn't afford to wait until the fuss died down.

'Okay.'

Tash was used to being looked at. She had no illusions about being any kind of a beauty, but—cosseted and nurtured on all that was good and nourishing by a mother who'd nearly lost her—she'd developed from a skin-and-bones kid into an unfashionably curved lushness that men seemed to find irresistible.

She'd quickly learned to keep both flirtatious vendors and buyers at a distance, but Darius Hadley had not flirted with her. The connection was something else, something visceral, and now he was looking at her with an intensity that heated her to the bone.

With each stroke of his pencil on the paper she became increasingly conscious of her body. Every line he drew felt like a fingertip stroked across her skin. It was as if she was coming undone; not just her top button, but every part of her was unravelling as she became exposed to him.

Far from keeping her distance, she'd barely stopped herself from reaching out, laying her hand on the solid muscle of his arm, sliding a finger along the dark hair gathered in a line along his forearm. But one touch would never be enough; it would be lighting the blue touchpaper, setting off a chain reaction that nothing could stop. And the problem with that was...?

'Did you hear me? I said okay.'

'Okay?' The breath hitched in her throat as she repeated the word. He'd agreed? 'Is that okay as in yes?' she asked. 'You'll give me a chance?'

There was a seemingly endless pause and for a moment he seemed to be somewhere else. Possibly thinking of all the reasons why it was a bad idea. What his lawyer would say. It would undoubtedly compromise his case against Morgan and Black...

'A conditional yes.'

Uh-oh...

'I'll give you a chance to sell Hadley Chase on one condition.'

'Anything,' she said.

'You're that desperate?' he asked, with a look that warned her she should have asked what condition.

'Anything that's legal, decent and honest,' she said, scarcely daring to breathe. Make that legal and honest. She was prepared to negotiate on decent...

'Desperate, but not stupid.'

Probably... 'What is it?'

'I want you to sit for me.'

'Sit?' For a moment she couldn't think what he meant but, as he continued to look at her, hold her fixed to the spot with no more than the power of his gaze, she knew exactly what he meant.

Her mouth dried and her hand fluttered from her shoulder to somewhere around her thigh in a gesture that took in all the important bits in between.

'As in *sit*?' she asked. 'Pose? Model for you?'

'If you're asking whether I'd want you naked, the answer is yes,' he said bluntly. 'It's your body that I want to draw, not your clothes.'

'Oh…' She blinked as a rush of blood heated her skin, her lips, and something deep within her liquefied. Appalled by how much she wanted to do it, she curled her fingers into her palms to stop herself from reaching for her buttons right then and there.

Misunderstanding her silence, he said, 'You're asking me to take you on trust, Natasha. That's a two-way deal.'

'Trust is important,' she agreed, 'but the thing is, I'm not asking you to take your clothes off.'

'I will if it will make it easier for you,' he said.

'Yes… No!' What on earth was she thinking? It was outrageous. She should be outraged, not tingling with excitement at the thought of exposing her ample curves to his molten gaze. So much for keeping this professional… 'Would you have asked if I was a man?'

He shrugged. 'Possibly. The right man, one with more than good muscle definition to commend him, and, like you, Natasha, he would have assumed I wanted more than a model.'

'I'm assuming nothing,' she declared, despite the betraying heat lighting up her cheeks that an artist, a man who saw more than most, would pick up in an instant, 'but I've just been handed a very painful lesson about mixing business with pleasure.' He said nothing so she continued. 'My fault. I broke the work/life balance golden rule.'

'With Morgan?' he asked.

'Miles? Good grief, no!'

'Then it has to be Toby Denton, the guy who's occupying your desk, driving your car. Did he get a hat-trick?'

'I'm sorry?'

'Did he break your heart, too?'

'Oh… No…' She shook her head. 'We didn't have that kind of a relationship.'

'What was it like?'

'A bit like a starter home,' she said. 'Something you know you're going to grow out of sooner rather than later. I was too busy for anything serious and, while he might look like perfect boyfriend material, there aren't many women who will play second fiddle to a rugby ball. The occasional night out, plus one do, sleepover suited us both.'

'Colleagues with benefits? It was still a betrayal.'

'Yes.' Worse, she would never know whether it had been a spur-of-the-moment thing or planned from the start and she had been duped, taken for a fool.

'Well, thanks for the vote of confidence,' he said after a moment, 'but sitting isn't a pleasure. It's uncomfortable, tedious, muscle-aching work. And you're right. Business and pleasure is a bad combination. Good models are hard to find, which is why I don't complicate the relationship with sex.'

'Does that mean…' She stopped. Of course it did. He'd just said so. Which was good. Really good. 'Can I see?' she asked, holding out her hand for the sketch pad, no longer so knicker-wettingly eager to get her kit off. 'What you've drawn?'

He handed it over without a word and she studied the small details he'd put down with little more than the stroke of a pencil.

Her mouth, fuller, sexier than she'd ever seen in the mirror when she'd grabbed a second to slide lipstick over it. The curve of her neck emerging from her collar, the line of her leg, her skirt stretched across her backside as she'd bent to search the fridge for milk—it was definitely time to get on the treadmill. Her eyes, giving away the feelings that vibrated through her whenever she looked at him.

'I understand why some primitive people thought the

camera stole away their soul,' she said, shaken by what he'd seen in those few moments, fixed on paper with so few lines. How much more would he see if he was being serious? She would be utterly exposed—and not just because she'd be stripped to her skin. 'It's not what I was expecting.'

Darius leaned back against the stepladder, folding his arms. 'Did you imagine I was drawing your internal organs?'

She swallowed, managed a wry smile. 'Well, that is more your style. This is just me.'

'What's on the surface. The image you show the world. I'll go deeper.'

'You won't find much muscle definition,' she warned him.

'You have a lot of everything, Natasha.'

'I was sick as a kid,' she said. 'My mother spent my childhood trying to fatten me up. I ran away from home to escape the egg custard.' She glanced up at the skeletal horse, then at the sketch pad, flipping back through the pages to see what else was there—anything to avoid looking at him, betray her eagerness for him to draw her, sculpt her—and discovered that every page was filled with drawings of her. Far more than he could have done in a few minutes. 'I don't understand. You couldn't have done all this today.'

'No.' His face was expressionless.

'But the other day... You only saw me for a minute or two and this is—'

'I've only scratched the surface.'

The room seemed to darken as their gazes locked, acknowledging the raw, subliminal connection in that moment when they'd faced one another across Morgan's office.

A shiver ran through her and she closed her eyes. When she opened them again, the sun was pouring in through the skylights and Darius was still waiting for her answer. He knew it would be yes...

'Will I be a limited edition bronze?' she asked. 'On display in a gallery window? Like the horse.'

'It's possible. If your interior lives up to the promise of the packaging.'

'My packaging!'

'It's very attractive packaging.'

'An excessive amount of packaging, I think you just said. Will you give me a couple of months to shed ten pounds?'

'Don't even think about it,' he said, taking the pad from her. 'Are you concerned that you'll be recognised?'

'Recognised?' The tension evaporated as she laughed at the idea of any of his subjects being recognised in the finished sculpture. 'Unlikely, I'd have thought.' She hoped. If anyone found out, she knew what interpretation they'd put on it. 'I might have to make it a condition.'

'It's all about trust,' he said, not joining in, and for a moment she was afraid that she'd offended him. 'So? Do you have any more problems?'

Problems?

Only one. The fact that she was more interested in the man than his house. She'd forgotten why she was here, that her future depended on getting this right. That problem.

'How about the fact that you'll be making money out of your side of the bargain while I'll be working for nothing?' she suggested in an attempt to bring them both back to the reason she was here.

'We might both be wasting our time, Natasha,' he said, pushing away from the stepladder, suddenly much too close. 'But if I discover depths in you that are worth exploring I'll...' His eyes suggested that his thoughts were a long way from art.

'Yes?' The word was thick in her throat. Not just his thoughts—her own were on a much lower plane...

'I'll give you a first casting.'

'So that I can put my "depths" on the sideboard for everyone I know to look at?'

'You'll love every minute of it,' he said. 'All those horny men running their hands over cold bronze, imagining the warm, living flesh.'

'No...' There was only one man she wanted running his hands over her flesh and he was right there, in front of her.

'Every woman longs for something in her past with which to scandalise her grandchildren,' he said. His face was all shadows, his eyes leaden, his voice so soft that it was barely audible.

'How would you know that?' she whispered.

He lifted his hand in what felt like slow motion and grazed her cheek with the roughened tips of his fingers and, as he drew them down the line of her jaw, a jolt went through her body as if it had been jump-started.

Her nipples tightened, puckering visibly beneath the heavy silk of her shirt, sending twin arrows of heat to the apex of her thighs, a bead of sweat trickled down her back and Darius, his thumb teasing the corner of her mouth, smiled darkly.

Question asked and answered.

She was finding it difficult to breathe, speech was beyond her; they both knew that she couldn't wait to have her depths thoroughly explored in every conceivable way, so she did the only thing left to her.

He didn't take his eyes from her face as she slipped the tiny pearl buttons of her shirt one by one until the silk parted and then, her eyes never leaving his, her parted lips swollen, burning, she turned her head to suck his thumb into her mouth.

Her tongue swirled around it, licking it, tasting clay and cake, sugar and something spicy that hadn't come out of a jar. She whimpered when he took it from her. Whimpered again when he dragged its moist, broad pad across her lips.

'Shush...' he murmured and there was a moment of perfect stillness when the world centred on that small contact, balanced on a knife-edge. Then he slowly lowered his mouth to hers, retraced the path of his thumb with his tongue and she nearly fainted from the hot burst of pleasure that flooded through her. It was only his arm supporting her that kept her on her feet as her lips parted and his tongue embarked on a meltingly slow dance of exploration.

She reached for him, cradling his head as the kiss deepened and her senses were bombarded from all directions. His hair tangled in her fingers, stubble tickled her palms. The scent of metal and clay and the oiled wooden handles of the tools he used clung to him, earthy and elemental. His hands tugged her shirt from her waistband and slid up her back, his thumbs nudged her breasts. The hard bulge of his erection butted into her hip.

He leaned back to look at her as he swept aside silk and lace, his calloused fingers lifting her breasts free of her bra, grazing the tender skin. And then his tongue swept over the rock-hard tip of her breast and her knees buckled.

There was a crash as he swept bones, tools aside and, without apparent effort, lifted her bodily onto the bench.

Yes...

The word spiralled through her, triumphant, exhilarating, liberating. She might have shouted it, but all she could hear was the sound of blood pounding in her ears as her pulse went off the scale. All she could feel was the heat of his mouth trailing moist kisses down her throat, his teeth, razor stubble grazing the swollen, sensitive skin of her breast, his suckling tongue sending a lightning bolt to her throbbing, swollen core.

'Darius...' It was a breathless, desperate plea and his hand was between her thighs, pushing aside the flimsy barrier to greet the liquid fire that flashed to meet first one and then two of those deliciously long fingers driving into her.

She reared to meet them, wanting more, demanding more as the furnace, lit in the very first moment she'd set eyes on him, hit meltdown. She'd wanted it then, wanted it as she'd beaten butter and sugar into submission, wanted him inside her...

She clutched at hard shoulders, her nails digging into his flesh through the soft cloth of his shirt as his knuckle hit the sweet, screaming spot. She had no breath to scream, urge him on; all she could do was make small desperate sounds as she arched upwards, demanding more, as he made her wait, taking his time, stroking, tormenting, teasing her throat, her breasts, her stomach with his teeth, his tongue, keeping her on the limit of endurance with his fingers, the subtle pressure of his thumb until her body, lost in bliss, slipped from her control and became entirely his. Only then did he release her in a shattering orgasm that went through her like a tornado, lifting, spinning, dumping her dazed, slicked with sweat and clinging to him like a life raft.

Her head was a dead weight against his shoulder, her limbs like sun-warmed putty, and if he hadn't been holding her she would have slithered to the floor in a boneless heap.

CHAPTER FIVE

FOR A LONG moment the only things moving in the room were dust motes dancing in the sunlight streaming in from above. Then Darius eased back a little.

'Are you okay?' he asked.

Okay? *Okay*?

'Give me a minute to locate my bones and I'll let you know.'

'Hang on…' He slid an arm beneath her knees and, lifting her clear of the bench, carried her to the sofa.

'Mmm…' She let out a contented sigh as she stretched out on the cushions, looking up at him from beneath lids too heavy to lift. She reached for his belt, planning to hook her fingers under it and pull him closer so that she could get at that deliciously flat belly beneath the baggy T-shirt, do a little nibbling on her own account. Ease the pressure of what had to be a very painful bulge against the zip of his jeans.

He caught her, wrapping his hand around her wrist, keeping her from her goal.

His eyes were burning her up and he held her tightly for a moment before, with a visible effort, he released her and then, taking care not to let his fingers touch her skin, lifted the lace of her bra and carefully replaced it over her breasts.

'Darius?'

He didn't answer but began to refasten her shirt buttons

with all the concentration of a bomb disposal officer defusing an unexploded bomb. One wrong move, one touch…

'What are you doing?' she demanded. Then, as the reality began to sink in, 'No…'

'I work here, Natasha, and I meant it when I said I don't have sex with my models.'

'I'm not a model…'

'No.' A faint smile tugged at the corner of his mouth. 'A professional model would never undress in front of an artist but, unless you're carrying a stash of condoms in that bag, we're done.'

The implication that she went to work armed and ready for action was like a bucket of cold water. Did he think she did that with everyone who needed a little encouragement to use her services?

Well, why wouldn't he? He knew she was desperate— desperate enough to sit naked so that he could draw her.

She'd completely lost the plot, forgotten that this was just business…

'Sorry,' she said, swinging her legs to the floor and forcing him to step back. 'You're not the only one who doesn't get down and dirty on the job,' she said, frustration making her snippy. 'Sex with a client is definitely off the agenda.'

'Just as well I'm not a client, then. Unless you've changed your mind about waiving your fee for selling the Chase?'

'No,' she said. 'A deal's a deal. I'll settle for the perks.'

'Perks?'

'The chunk of bronze to go on the mantelpiece, the hand job. Thanks for that, by the way; it's been too long…' The words were out before her brain was engaged… 'Give me a call when you want me to strip naked for you,' she added, putting some stiffeners in her legs so that she could stand up. Get out of there. 'You'll find my number inside the lid of the cakebox.'

'Most people find a business card more convenient,' he

said, flipping it open and glancing at the label on which she'd printed her name, telephone number and email address as he searched for a phone amongst the scattered tools and bones on his workbench and programmed in the number. 'You can carry more than one at a time.'

'Unfortunately, my card is out of date and since I had no way of knowing if you'd listen to me...' She swallowed. He'd done a lot more than listen and she'd done a lot more than talk. 'In my experience, men don't throw away home-made cake, no matter where it's come from.'

'You were confident that once I'd tasted it I'd want more?'

The scent of sex hung in the air as thick as paint and they both knew that the taste he was referring to had nothing to do with confectionery.

No, no, no... 'Oh, please!' she said. 'When I have all those horny men queuing up at my front door for my lemon drizzle.'

Take that, Mr Hadley...

'Really?' He sucked on the tip of his thumb. 'Personally, I prefer my sugar light on the lemon, heavy on the spice.' A hot flush raced from her navel to her scalp as she realised that he was tasting her. 'Sticky ginger...' he said, volley intercepted and returned. Point won... 'I've sent you my number. In case you run into any problems.'

'Problems. Right.' There wouldn't be any problems. She'd make sure of that. But first she had to get out of here before she spontaneously combusted.

Jacket...

Where was it?

She looked around, knowing that she should be grateful that she wasn't crawling around on her hands and knees looking for her underwear.

She should.

Really.

Darius spotted her jacket lying on the floor beside the sofa and, beating Natasha to it, scooped it up. She took a nervous step back, keeping him at arm's length. She was mad at him. The condom remark had been crass, deliberately so—a bucket of cold water on an overheated situation that had got out of hand. Unfortunately, all it had done was create steam. They were both still on a hair trigger and playing Russian roulette which was why, instead of following her excellent example and tossing it to her, he shook her jacket out and held it up, inviting her to turn around and slide her arms into the sleeves.

She could have ignored him, said she'd carry it, but after the slightest hesitation she turned, holding her arms towards him so that he could ease it on. She smelled of spice and sex and, with a groan he couldn't stifle, he slid his hands down from her shoulders to cup her lovely breasts, pulling her against him while he breathed a kiss against her neck. She leaned back into him with a whimper that was half despair, half bliss and for a moment he just held her, before summoning the willpower to give her a gentle push towards the door.

'Go,' he said.

She turned in his arms and looked up at him, her eyes liquid, appealing.

'Now,' he said, his forehead touching hers, her breasts brushing against his chest. He was wood and there was nothing he could do about it. 'Please.'

She took a breath. 'Right. Yes… This was so not what I intended.' She took a step back, picked up her bag, made it as far as the door, then paused. 'I won't bother you again until I have some news.'

'I won't be holding my breath.'

Wrong on both counts.

He'd been bothered the minute he'd set eyes on her. Unable to get her out of his mind. And breathless ever since she'd walked into his studio with that mesmerising sway of her hips.

'How will you get there?' he asked. A tiny frown puckered her smooth forehead. 'The Chase. Now that the devious Denton is driving your Beemer?'

'Oh...' She shook her head, as if clearing it. 'I'll hire something.'

'A waste of money. You'd be better off putting a deposit on a van,' he said. 'That way you can put your name on the side and use it as free advertising. Sell the house and I'll design you a logo.'

Things were safer than feelings...

'If I sell the house,' she pointed out, 'I won't need one.'

'If you sell the house, Natasha, you won't need to work for anyone else. It won't only be eager estate agents, and horny men pining for you, but desperate vendors who'll be beating a path to your door.'

'Thanks, but self-employment doesn't figure in my five-year career plan.'

'I think we've established that right now you don't have a career or a plan.'

'The career is temporarily on hold. The plan is a work in progress,' she said and, as if to underline the fact that—perks notwithstanding—this was strictly business, she offered him her hand.

Despite the danger to his simmering libido, he was unable to resist taking it. Small, soft, with perfectly groomed nails, it lay like a touch of velvet against his clay-roughened palm evoking X-rated thoughts and he needed to get her out of his studio before common sense went to hell in a hand basket.

'Please go,' he said.

Her lips parted as if she was going to say something. Clearly she thought better of it and, having opened the door, she stepped through into the street and closed it behind her without another word.

He slipped the latch before Patsy decided to pop in and give him the third degree, leaning his forehead against it while he called the estate executor to update him on the situation.

Brian Ramsey spluttered and protested at the inappropriateness of allowing Natasha access to the house, but Darius cut him short.

'You chose Morgan and Black to handle the sale. They messed up,' he said. 'Now we'll do it my way. Please make sure that Gary Webb is available tomorrow to let her in.'

'Mr Webb is on sick leave and really, in the light of recent events, I have to insist that Miss Gordon is accompanied by someone responsible. Tell her that if she comes in the office later this week I'll check the diary and see when someone is available.'

Oh, right. Next month some time. Maybe. This was the man who'd conspired with his grandfather to ensure that a Hadley remained at the Chase for another generation.

'What's the matter with Gary?' he asked.

'He had a fall.'

Tash walked away on legs that were all over the place, her stomach churning with every kind of emotion imaginable.

She needed to sit down. Needed coffee. Ice cream…

For heaven's sake, she was a grown-up and smart enough to know that leaping on a man you barely knew was never going to end well, especially when it was supposed to be strictly business. *Especially* when her entire life plan depended on it being strictly business.

What on earth had she been thinking?

Scratch that. No one had been thinking, least of all her. Apparently she still wasn't because she couldn't wait for the return match and next time she'd have more than cake in her bag...

She was grinning, helplessly, at the thought when her phone began to ring. She checked the number, ultra cautious since her name had been plastered all over the evening papers. Journalists might believe that she was safely tucked up out of harm's way in the Fairview where they couldn't get at her, but it hadn't stopped them trying her number, leaving sympathetic messages, wanting her side of the story. As if she was going to fall for that.

It wasn't a journalist. It was Darius.

'Text me your address,' he said, before her brain could unscramble itself and deliver a simple hello.

'Excuse me?'

'The caretaker is in hospital and the legal lot insist that you're accompanied by a responsible adult.'

'That's very, um, responsible of them.' She'd bet the house that wasn't all they'd said. They would have had a dozen good reasons why he should pull out of their deal. Given a minute, she could probably come up with at least that many herself. But he hadn't... 'What's the matter with Mr Grumpy?'

'He fell off a ladder. Broken leg, broken wrist, bruises.'

'Oh...' How to go from feeling great to feeling about two inches high in ten seconds. 'I'm so sorry.' And she was. He'd been a grouch but he didn't deserve that. 'Is he going to be okay?' Then, as an awful thought struck her, she said, 'He wasn't trying to fix that window, was he?'

'Is that a guilty conscience I can hear, Miss Gordon?' Darius asked. 'Maybe you should take him some of your cake.'

'Darius!'

He laughed. 'Relax, Sugarlips. This is not your fault—he was clearing a blocked gutter at the village hall, but you're right, it needs fixing. I'll get it sorted.'

Sugarlips? Oh, cripes…

'I could arrange that for you,' she offered, doing her best not to think about what had made him pick on that particular endearment. She should definitely not think about him sucking the tip of his thumb. She could still taste him, smell him on her… 'I have a first-class honours degree in estate management.'

'Well, bully for you. Call the National Trust; maybe they'll give you a job.'

'They did,' she said. 'I turned it down.'

There was a brief silence which told her that she'd finally managed to surprise him, then he said, 'I'll pick you up at eight tomorrow morning.'

'You?'

'I'm the only responsible adult available at short notice.'

'Oh…' Her heart, already going like the clappers, hit warp speed.

'Of course you could wait for Brian Ramsey to find some free time in his diary but he isn't particularly happy with my choice of sales agent so he won't be in any hurry.'

'No, thanks. I talked to Brian Ramsey about cleaning up the house. He was barely polite when I was representing an agency he had engaged.'

'Then I'll see you tomorrow. You can bring lunch.'

'Blokes do windows, women do food?'

'You could take me to the pub if you'd prefer, but I was thinking of your budget.'

'A picnic it is. Any allergies?' she asked. 'Anything you won't eat?'

'Just save the wussy lemon cake for your legions of admirers. You know what I like.'

He disconnected before she could reply and Tash had to fight the insane urge to run back to the studio and write her address in lipstick on his sketch pad. On his chest. Across his stomach…

'Are you all right, dear?' A woman waiting for the bus was looking up at her with concern.

'Um… Yes… Thank you.' She sat down on the bench beside her, flapped her shirt collar to create a bit of breeze around her face. 'I've just, um… It's a bit warm, isn't it?'

Darius was at the door on the dot of eight and despite a sleepless night—or maybe because of it—Tash was waiting for him. No short skirt, no dangerous buttons with a mind of their own, no sexy high heels. Today she was kitted out in a pair of comfortable jeans, a baggy T-shirt and a pair of running shoes, bought when she'd decided to get a grip on her weight and decided to go running with Toby. Once had been enough and any wear on the soles was down to the occasional dash to the corner shop for emergency baking supplies.

Her laptop bag was ready for business, lunch was packed; she hadn't left herself with a single excuse to delay so that she would have to invite him up while she gathered her stuff. No excuse to offer him coffee, or invite him to try the spiced cookies she'd been baking at three that morning.

There was work to do, her career to save, Hadley Chase to sell and when he buzzed from the front entrance she was ready to go.

Strictly business.

She ran down the stairs, swung through the door…

Oh, good grief.

He didn't say anything when she skidded to a stop on the pavement and the casual *hi* that she'd been mentally rehearsing died on her lips at the sight of him leaning back against the door of an elderly Land Rover.

If the vehicle was well past its prime, Darius, in a black polo shirt and faded denims that clung to his thighs, was looking like every kind of sin she'd ever wanted to commit.

He was just so damned beautiful that every one of her

nerve endings sent out a 'touch me' tingle and she was seriously wishing she'd gone for a shirt with unreliable buttons and a bra that pushed her boobs up to her chin. He
might keep a poker face when he was looking down her
cleavage but she knew exactly what he was thinking. Right
now she hadn't a clue.

She'd run through this moment over and over as she was
taking a shower, picking out what to wear for exploring a
dusty old house, cutting sandwiches. Imagining what he'd
say, what he'd do. Rehearsing every possible combination
of responses.

Would it be a curt let's-forget-what-happened nod? Emi-
nently sensible...

Her heart had skipped a little beat at the prospect of a
let's-think-about-this kiss on the cheek. Sensible but with
possibilities...

Or please, please, please, a let's-do-it kiss that would
buckle her knees and have her melting on the pavement.

None of the above.

He kept his distance, one eyebrow slightly raised as he
took in her passion-damping clothes, her hair fastened in a
single plait that was held together with nothing sexier than
an elastic band. Then, just when she thought it was safe to
breathe, he reached out, ran his thumb over her mouth and
said, 'Good morning, Sugarlips.'

His low, sexy voice vibrated against her breastbone and
the carrier containing their lunch slipped through her fingers and hit the pavement.

An annoying little smile lifted the corner of his mouth
as he straightened and opened the passenger door. 'I hope
there was nothing breakable in there.'

'The flask is well padded, but I don't suppose it will
have done the cake much good,' she replied before, blushing like an idiot, she scrambled up into the passenger seat,
leaving him to pick it up.

She concentrated on fastening her seat belt as he climbed in beside her, filling the space with his presence, his earthy scent mingling with the smell of hot oil.

Her fingers were shaking so much that he took her hand, unpeeled her fingers from it and clicked it home.

'It was a bit stiff…'

'I know how it feels.'

She tried not to look, but was unable to help herself. Oh, cripes…

'I'm sorry the transport doesn't meet your usual standard of comfort,' he said, leaning forward to start the engine, ignoring the tension twanging the air between them; presumably a man who spent his life around naked women posing on a pedestal would have had plenty of practice.

She made an effort to focus her thoughts elsewhere. On the house with the puce living room that had been on the market for months and the owner's outrage when she'd suggested that a quick coat of magnolia might help…

Her breathing slowed, the pulse pounding in her throat became a gentle thud.

Better.

'No problem,' she said. 'As you pointed out, I'm working this job economy class.'

'You've got it,' he said, a wry smile creating a crease in his cheek and undoing all that effort. Fortunately the Land Rover, vibrating noisily, covered the shiver that rippled through her.

'So, what's the plan?' he said.

'Plan?'

'I assumed you'd been up half the night working on your plan to find a buyer for the Chase.'

'It shows, huh?' The expensive stuff that was supposed to conceal dark shadows round the eyes clearly wasn't doing the job.

'Just guessing,' he said, ratcheting up the smile, and

the swarm of butterflies in her stomach, which until then had at least been flying in close formation, went haywire.

Think about that hideous purple and yellow bathroom...

'Nearly right,' she managed. 'I was up half the night creating a media presence for Hadley Chase on Facebook and Twitter.'

Nearly right. Nearly true. She'd done that within half an hour of getting home. The major time had been spent finding and following media types—and the people they followed—journalists, the local Berkshire newspapers and county magazine. Anyone who had an interest in country houses, property, local history, social history. Anyone who might conceivably be interested in following Hadley Chase.

She'd spent the rest of the night trying to come up with a really convincing reason why she should call him and cancel. She needed to keep her distance, keep it professional.

She also needed to get to Hadley Chase this week, rather than at the convenience of a lawyer who thought she was poison, so here she was, on the dot of eight o'clock, her brain out to lunch and her stomach throwing a butterfly party while she drooled over the man.

Forget strictly business. She should have lured him up to her flat and invited him to shag her brains out. Maybe then she'd be able to concentrate on the job in hand.

He glanced back over his shoulder, giving his attention to the traffic. Giving her a moment to catch her breath.

She focused on the memory of a house with an orange front door. And that had been the best bit. A kitchen with every tile on both walls and floor a different colour. Heard herself saying, 'So jolly...'

Maybe he wasn't as cool as he looked either and needed a moment of his own because he didn't press her on the plan. Which was just as well. She wasn't getting paid so she couldn't afford to throw money at the problem; she was going to have to be inventive.

'How's Mr Gr...er...Gary?' she said, raising her voice above the noise of the engine when the silence had gone on too long.

'Comfortable, according to the nurse I spoke to.'

'I'm really sorry.'

'Not half as sorry as he is, I suspect.'

'I meant I'm sorry that you have to do this. You didn't want to be involved. In the sale.'

They were stopped in traffic and he looked across at her as if unsure how to answer her. His eyes were liquid silver in the morning sunlight, with a hint of steely blue. Then someone hooted impatiently from behind and once they were rattling along the motorway the noise of the engine, the tyres, the trucks rushing past, made anything but the most urgent conversation impossible.

Tash made an effort to focus on the problem ahead—she had no illusions about the Chase being an easy sell—but she was sitting within inches of Darius Hadley. Sunlight was glinting over the steel wristband of his watch, drawing attention to the hand wrapped lightly around the steering wheel, the fingers that had been inside her, driving her wild with pleasure less than twenty-four hours ago.

Who could focus on anything but the mesmerising flex of the muscles in his forearm, his thigh as he changed gear, switched lanes?

Swamped by lust, heated by the sun beating in through the windscreen on her breasts, thighs, she closed her eyes to shut out temptation. When she opened them again, her cheek was pressed against his shoulder, she was breathing in the scent of warm male and her first inclination was to close them and stay exactly where she was.

She felt, rather than saw, Darius glance down at her. 'It must have been a late night. Not many people can sleep in a Land Rover.'

Humbled, she reluctantly straightened. 'I was just resting

my eyes,' she said, using a yawn to surreptitiously check her chin for dribble. 'While I focused on the plan.'

'Sure you were,' he said, grinning.

'The brain does its best work while the subconscious is switched off,' she said, realising that they'd left the motorway. How long had she slept?

Her satnav had kept her on the main roads but Darius, on home ground, had ignored the dual carriageway that bypassed the village of Hadley and as she looked around, trying to figure out where they were, he slowed and turned down a track half hidden by the rampant growth of early summer spilling from the verges.

'I hope we don't meet anyone coming the other way,' she said as they bounced, very slowly, through a tunnel of fresh new summer leaves along a dirt track so narrow that the frothy billow of cow parsley brushed both the sides of the Land Rover.

'If we do, they'd better have a good reason for being here,' he said. 'This is estate land.'

'This is the back way in?' she asked, trying to recall a map she'd seen, orientate herself. A chalk stream, low after an unusually dry spring, was curling quietly around shingle banks just below them on the right, which put them at the lower end of the estate and, as she turned and looked up, she caught a glimpse of tall chimneys through a gap in the trees.

'The main road goes round in a long loop to bypass the village,' he said. 'This entrance is known only to estate residents, who have more respect for their suspension than to use it, and locals doing a little rough shooting for the pot.'

She looked at him. 'Do you mean poachers?'

'My grandfather would have called them that,' he said. 'I don't have a problem with the neighbours keeping the pigeon and rabbit population under control in return for the odd trout.'

'Well, that's very neighbourly, but people who buy this kind of property tend to be nervous of unidentified gunfire,' she said, trying to pin down what exactly was wrong with the way he said 'grandfather'. 'If…when…I find you a buyer, someone had better warn the locals that they'll have to find their small game somewhere else.'

His jaw tightened, but all he said was, 'I'll make sure Gary passes the word. When…if…you find a buyer. Having burned the midnight oil and spent the drive down here leaving the work to your subconscious,' he said, 'have you got any further than creating a Facebook page?'

'It's a work in progress,' she admitted. Between reliving their close encounter in his studio and wondering how soon they could manage a replay, she hadn't been giving nearly enough thought to saving her career. 'What I need is a story.'

'A story?' He slowed almost to a stop, looking at her instead of the track.

'Relax, Darius, I've got the message. Your name is off limits. Cross my heart,' she added and then, as his eyes darkened, she drew her finger, very slowly, across her left breast in a large X.

His foot slipped from the accelerator, the engine stalled and only the ticking of the engine disturbed a silence so thick that it filled her ears.

'You are in so much trouble, Natasha Gordon,' he said, his face all dark shadows, his eyes shimmering with heat.

'Is that a promise?' she asked, her breath catching in her throat. 'Or are you all talk?'

The click of their seat belts being released was like a shotgun in the silence and then his hands were on her waist and, without quite knowing how she'd got there, she was straddling his thighs, her mouth a breath away from lips that had haunted her since the moment she'd first seen him.

She wiggled a little, snuggling her backside closer to the

impressive bulge in his jeans, and he groaned. 'Correction. *I'm* in so much trouble…'

'Talk, talk, talk…' she murmured against his mouth, cutting off any attempt at a response with a swirl of her tongue over his lower lip. There was a satisfying buck from his hips and, giving no quarter, she sucked it into her mouth.

Darius leaned back to give her more room.

There had been a bulge in his pants ever since she'd appeared on her doorstep in curve-disguising clothes, her hair in restraints, minimal make-up. She'd been doing her best to appear cool but she hadn't needed lipstick to draw attention to a mouth that had been hot, swollen, screaming *kiss me* at a hundred decibels.

He just about managed to restrain himself—if he'd kissed her they would never have left London and he wanted this over. He'd done a good job of keeping his mind on the road while he was driving along the motorway, but then she'd fallen asleep with her head against his shoulder, her lips slightly parted, wisps of escaping hair brushing his neck. Now the scent of hot woman was filling his lungs.

'You want action, Sugarlips?' he said. 'Help yourself.'

Needing no second invitation, she slid her hands through his hair, tangling it in her fingers, a little cat smile tugging at her lips as she made him her captive, teased him with her mouth, sucking, nipping, inviting him to come out and play.

He was in no hurry. Right now her breasts were snuggled against his chest, her backside was tormenting his erection, her mouth trailing moist kisses under his chin.

There was nothing more arousing than a woman intent on pleasure and, resting his hands on her hips, he did no more than support her, holding her steady so that she could concentrate on driving him wild.

It didn't take long. Her top, barely skimming her waistband, rode up as she leaned forward and he closed his eyes, memorising each curve of her lovely body as his hands, with a will of their own, slid up to graze the silk of her skin. Her waist dipped above the flare of her hips; there was nothing straight about her, he discovered, as his thumbs teased the edges of her stomach and she squirmed on his lap.

For a moment he was the one holding his breath but then he reached her ribcage and he felt the hitch of her breath under his hands as his fingers took a slow walk up her spinal column, kneading each vertebrae in turn, pausing only to release the catch on her bra, so that his thumbs were free to imprint the soft swell of her breasts in his memory. They had just reached her nipples when her tongue found the pulse throbbing in his neck.

With a roar, he pulled her top, bra over her head and tossed them behind him, then forgot to breathe as she leaned back against the steering wheel, eyes smoky, slumberous, only the tiniest rim of blue circling satin-black pupils.

'Perfect,' he said, filling his hand with her full, ripe breasts, thumbing her rock-hard nipples, stroking them with his tongue, sucking on them. Just perfect…

'Darius…' There was an urgency in her voice now and he popped the button at her waist, slid down the zip and eased his hands down inside the back of her jeans, a scrap of lace, easing them down as he cupped her peachy backside in his hands and lifted her towards his mouth.

He swirled his tongue around the dimple of her navel, mouthed soft kisses in the hollow of her pelvis, blew against the blonde fluff of her sex and she whimpered, wanting more. She was right—this wasn't enough. He wanted her naked. He wanted her out of here, lying on a bank of soft grass down by the stream with sunlight, filtered through the leaves, playing on her skin. He wanted to touch every inch of her, memorise her body. Be inside her…

'Let's get out of here,' he said, pushing open the door

and half falling with her into the verge, where they lay laughing, catching their breath amongst long grass, red campion, a few late bluebells that were a perfect match for her eyes. 'Come on,' he said, hauling her up, holding her close, not wanting to let her go even for the short scramble down the bank.

She clutched at jeans that were heading for her knees. 'Where are we going?'

'You're not going anywhere.'

'What the…?' He swung round and Natasha gave a little shriek as they were confronted by a helmeted, visored security guard. 'Where the hell did you come from?' he demanded.

Ignoring his question, the guard said, 'This is private property. You're going to have to leave.'

'What? No…' Then cursed himself for every kind of fool—Ramsey had told him that he'd employed a security firm to keep an eye on the place. Cursed again as he realised that Natasha was standing there without a stitch above her waist and not much below it and putting himself between them. 'Show a little respect,' he said, boiling with anger that the man hadn't had the decency to look away. More likely couldn't take his eyes off her.

Despite his helmet and a uniform designed to make him look as much like a policeman as possible without breaking the law, the man took a nervous step back, looked away.

'There's no need for that,' he said defensively. 'I'm just doing my job.'

'Hanging about like some Peeping Tom. You're the trespasser,' he said, wrenching off his polo shirt and handing it to Natasha, bundling her back into the seat they'd just fallen out of before turning furiously on the man. 'This is my land.' The words were out of his mouth before he realised what he was saying. 'I am Darius Hadley and I own this estate.'

'Good try, but Mr Hadley is dead,' he replied, 'and the house is being sold, so if you'd just get back in the vehicle. You can turn around about fifty yards ahead—'

'I know where I can turn. I know every inch of this estate,' he said, cutting him off, but clearly words weren't going to do it. Taking his wallet from his back pocket, he opened it and held it out so that the man could see his driver's licence. 'Darius Hadley,' he repeated, while the man checked the name and photograph. 'The previous owner was my grandfather.'

'Even so, sir, I'll have to check with the office.'

'Check with who you like. How did you know we were here?' It seemed unlikely that a patrol just happened to be passing at the exact moment he'd stalled his engine.

'There's CCTV on all the entrances, Mr Hadley. Apparently this one is something of a lovers'...'

'Get rid of it.'

'I'm sorry...'

'I want the cameras down now. Every one of them, is that clear?'

'I can't—'

Darius didn't wait for the excuses, but reached into the Land Rover for his mobile phone and called Brian Ramsey.

'Ramsey,' he said, before the man could do more than say his name, 'I understand that you've had security cameras installed at the Chase. Get rid of them. And the security company.'

'Darius...' he said, in what he no doubt thought was a soothing voice. 'The house is empty and this is the most economic...'

'It's intrusive. The tenants have a right to privacy.'

'I'm sure if you asked them they would tell you that there have been problems with trespassers, poachers. The trout stream is a selling point and the insurance company...'

'There's a public footpath across the estate and those

poachers are not just keeping down the rabbit population, they're local people and they do a better job of keeping an eye on the place than any security firm. No arguments. I own this estate and I want the cameras gone. Today.'

He ended the call without waiting to hear more and turned to the man. 'You heard me. You're fired.'

CHAPTER SIX

'ARE YOU OKAY?'

'There's nothing wrong with me,' Natasha said as Darius climbed in beside her. 'You could do with a few lessons in reality, though.'

'What?' About to reach for the ignition, he sat back, dragged his fingers through his hair. Far from okay, she was furious. 'I'm sorry. That was—'

'Don't apologise to me,' she snapped. 'What on earth were you thinking?'

He glanced at her, aware that he was missing something but not sure what. 'I was thinking that perhaps you might just be a little bit upset at being seen half-naked by a total stranger,' he said.

'Really? And how would that be different from you making a bronze of my entirely naked body for the entire world to stare at?' He wasn't deceived by the mildness of her tone. She was mad and actually he didn't blame her. On a stupid scale of one to ten that had to be a nine. She might have been up there with him, reaching for ten, but he'd started it. Clearly some serious grovelling was in order, but she wasn't done. 'I am not made of porcelain, Darius; I won't break if some bloke gets an eyeful of my tits, but that man probably has a wife and family to support.'

What? He was apologising to her, but apparently her only concern was some lout who'd leered at her breasts.

'How do you suppose his employers will react when they're told they've lost their contract because someone— a man who was just doing his job keeping Hadley Chase safe from intruders—hacked off the high and mighty Darius Hadley?'

High and mighty?

'I'm not—'

'No? You should have *heard* yourself. *"This is my land!"* Really? Because I got the strong impression that you don't give a tuppenny damn about the place.'

'I give a damn,' he said.

'About selling it as quickly as possible with the least possible inconvenience to yourself.'

'No…'

'When was the last time you actually set foot on the place?'

'You have no idea—'

'So tell me.'

Tell her? What? That his father had sold him? Share the shrivelling knowledge that his value had been counted in sterling. That his grandfather had forced his own son to choose between the woman he loved beyond reason and his infant son.

He was still holding his cell phone and, instead of answering her, he hit redial.

'Ramsey…I'm sorry,' he began before the man had a chance to say more than his name. 'You're right, the house must have a security presence and the company are doing an excellent job. Please ask them to pass on my apologies to the guard I met this morning. He took me by surprise but he was simply doing his job and it has been pointed out to me that I behaved like a jerk.'

He didn't wait for an answer, but disconnected, tossed the phone back on the shelf and reached for the ignition.

Natasha cleared her throat. 'Do you want your shirt back?'

'Keep it,' he said. 'I'll wear your top. Now you've cut me down to size, it'll be a perfect fit.'

'Oh, I think you fill this one pretty well,' she said, pulling it over her head and handing it to him, before turning behind to recover her top and bra from the back seat. By the time she was straight he had pulled up in front of the house.

To the right the parkland fell away to the river; then, beyond it, the Downs offered a breathtaking view for miles around.

Tash sighed. Beside her, Darius had that same locked-away look that he'd had when she'd first set eyes on him, except now she knew that it was not simply about the advertisement. For a moment, before he'd called Brian Ramsey, told him to apologise to the security guard, she'd seen the darkness, a pain like a knife in his heart.

There was something about this house, what had happened here, that hurt bone-deep, and yet he'd brought her here. She'd like to think it was because he wanted to spend the day with her, maybe fool around a little—fool around a lot if the last few minutes were anything to go by. Now she realised that she had simply provided him with a hook, that her need had given him an excuse, a way back.

The minute he came to a halt, she climbed down, grabbed her bags from the back seat but, instead of going straight to the door, she walked to the edge of the lawn where there was a strategically placed bench, giving him breathing space to come to terms with being here before he had to go inside.

Meanwhile, she had a job to do and she'd better jolly well stop lusting after Darius; she took out her mini camcorder and began to create a panorama to post on Facebook.

The crunch of his boots on the gravel warned her that he had followed her. 'The house might have a few shortcomings, but the setting is perfect,' she said, not looking up until the view was blocked by his broad chest. She didn't stop filming but, instead of panning from left to right, she lifted the lens until his face filled the screen.

'Here are the keys. The alarm code is 2605.'

'You're leaving me to it?' she asked, letting the camera fall to her side, a little hollow spot of disappointment somewhere below her waist that he was ducking out. 'I thought you'd been appointed responsible adult?'

'Apparently I failed at the first hurdle. Don't worry. I'll ask that security guard to frisk you for the family silver before you leave,' he said.

'You were wrong, Darius.'

'Totally.' He met her gaze head-on. 'I lashed out because I felt guilty.'

'I realise that, but I'm an adult; I knew where I was, what I was doing. The responsibility was equally mine.'

'But you didn't know what I knew.'

'Oh? And what was that?'

'Ramsey told me he'd employed a security company; it just never occurred to me that they would be monitoring the place so closely.' He shrugged, summoned up the ghost of a smile. 'Forget that; I wasn't thinking about anything except getting you naked.'

She resisted the urge to fling herself at him again and, keeping her own smile low-key, said, 'Ditto.'

His own smile deepened a fraction, but he shook his head.

'Shall I tell you why I liked being with Toby?' she asked.

'No—'

'He never patronised me,' she said. 'He never doubted that I knew what I was doing.' Okay, he wasn't that bright. If she knew what she was doing, she wouldn't be this close to a man who made her self-preservation hard drive crash whenever she thought about touching him. About him touching her. 'He never felt the need to protect me.'

'He stole your job!'

'He was paying me the ultimate compliment, Darius. He knew that I was strong enough, smart enough, to survive.'

'Maybe, but I wasn't patronising you. I was just doing that macho shit…'

'I know.' About to reach out, touch him, reassure him, she tucked the house keys in her pocket, sat down on the bench, took a flask out of her bag, keeping her hands busy.

She'd wanted him to share his pain. Maybe, while she had him on her hook, she could show him how.

'I spent the first twenty-one years of my life being protected, Darius. It gets old.' She unscrewed the cups from the top of the flask, looked up. 'Have you got time for coffee?'

Darius recognised his moment to make his excuses and walk away. It was what he always did when things became complicated, involved—walking away from emotional entanglement. Something he'd been signally failing to do ever since he'd set eyes on Natasha Gordon in Morgan's office.

He'd walked, but he'd hardly made it across the road before he was looking back, hooked on that luscious body, those eyes. Now, layered on that first explosive impact, was her sweet, spicy, delicious scent, the taste of her skin, her mouth entwining itself around him, binding him to her.

He should be running, not walking away, but he'd been running since he was seventeen years old. Running from the house behind him and yet here he was, because Natasha had needed him. Or maybe he'd needed the excuse she gave him to return, face it. Whichever it was, he barely hesitated before joining her on the bench, taking the coffee she'd poured for him.

'Thanks.'

'You're welcome,' she said, but didn't follow it up with an offer of something sweet to go with it. Just as well—

'cake' would, in his mind, forever be a euphemism for sex and even he balked at a garden bench with half an acre of lawn in front of them.

'Okay,' he said, 'I'm hooked. Tell me about the first twenty-one years of your life.'

'All of them?' she asked. 'I thought you had to be some-where.'

He leaned an elbow on the back of the bench, making it clear he was going nowhere. 'Hospital visiting.' Another hurdle to face. 'Gary isn't going anywhere.'

She took a sip of her coffee.

'Come on,' he said, waggling his eyebrows at her. 'You know you want to tell me.'

'But do you really want to hear?'

He was beginning to get a bad feeling about this, wishing he'd gone with his first thought and walked away. 'How about a quick rundown of the highlights?' he suggested.

'Lowlights would be more accurate,' she said.

'Were they that bad?'

'No…' She reached out as if to reassure him and for a moment her fingers brushed his arm. 'But highlights are all sparkle and excitement. Champagne and strawberries.'

'And lowlights are egg custard?'

She laughed. 'Give the man a coconut. My first twenty-one years were all wholesome, nourishing, good-for-you egg custard when I longed for spicy, lemony, chocolatey, covered-in-frosting, bad-for-you, sugar-on-the-lips cake,' she said.

'Thanks for the coconut, but I don't deserve it,' he said. 'I have absolutely no idea what you're talking about.'

'Of course not. No one ever does.'

'Try me.'

She looked at him over the rim of her cup, then put it down. 'Okay. It's taking quiet beach holidays in the same cottage with my family in Cornwall every year, when I dreamed of being in a hot-air balloon floating across the Serengeti, bungee jumping in New Zealand, white water rafting in Colorado like my brothers.'

'Why?'

'Given the choice, wouldn't you have preferred hot-air ballooning?'

He thought about it for a moment then said, 'Actually they both have a lot to commend them and Cornwall does have surfing.'

Tash, who was finding this a lot harder than she imagined, grabbed the distraction. 'You surf? In one of those clinging wetsuits?' She flapped a hand to wave cooling air over her face. 'Be still my beating heart.'

'You don't?' he asked, refusing to be distracted.

'Surf? I can't even swim. The most dangerous thing I do at the seaside is paddle up to my ankles with my nephews and nieces. Build sandcastles. Play shove ha'penny down the pub.'

'And again, why? You mentioned that you were sick as a kid, but you look pretty robust now.'

'Robust?' She rolled the word round her mouth, testing it. 'Thanks for that. It makes me feel so much better.'

'No need to get on your high horse; you have a great body—one that I guarantee would cause a riot in a wetsuit—but that wasn't the "why" I was asking. Why were your parents so protective?'

And suddenly there it was. She'd lived a lifetime with everyone knowing what had happened to her, looking at her with a touch of uncertainty, of pity.

She'd left all that behind when she'd left home. She hadn't told anyone in London, not even Toby, but when Miles had introduced a private health scheme for the staff late last year, the insurance company had put so many restrictions on her that he'd called her into his office, convinced she was a walking time bomb. She'd told him everything and now the bastard had used it against her.

Had it played on his mind when he was thinking of promoting her? Because it stayed with you, stuck like dog muck on a shoe. Telling Darius was harder than she'd imagined when she'd blithely set out to show him how to trust someone so totally that you exposed yourself in ways that had nothing to do with getting naked.

Their relationship was purely physical and she never saw it being anything else. He had 'loner' stamped all over him, but she didn't want to alter the image he had of her. To have the 'attractive packaging' undermined by that darkness he would find in her inner depths and exposed in bronze. But he'd given her his trust when not many men in his situation would have given her the time of day and if she could get him to open up she would have repaid him whether she sold Hadley Chase or not.

'I had cancer—' There it was, the great big nasty C-word. 'Leukaemia—'

'Leukaemia?' Well, that put a dent in his smile. 'Oh, God, I'm sorry. I thought…'

'What?'

'From what you said about being force-fed egg custard…'

'What?'

'The newspaper hinted at some psychological problem…' He looked distinctly uncomfortable. 'Patsy wondered if you might have had some kind of eating disorder.'

'You've got to be kidding!' The tension erupted in a burst of laughter. 'Look at me!'

Darius looked and he wanted to laugh, too. 'I told her she was way off beam,' he said. 'I'm beginning to have a very warm regard for egg custard.' His fingers lightly traced the outline of her face from temple to chin. 'That is a very healthy glow.'

'I think the word you're looking for is pink and over-weight,' she said, 'which actually is pretty ironic.'

'Pretty' was too bland a word for Natasha. She was no pretty milkmaid... 'It is?'

'I'm told that people suffering from anorexia look at themselves in the mirror and see fat even when they're skin and bones. Well, my parents look at me and see skin and bones despite the fact that I'm—'

'Luscious.'

'Nicely fielded,' she said, turning away, but he hooked his finger around her chin, forcing her to look him in the eyes.

'I know what I mean, Natasha.'

'Do you?'

'Believe me. I can usually wait to get a room.'

'Are you saying that you don't usually toss women into the nearest verge?' she teased, laughing now as the tension of telling her story left her and he added a whole raft of other words to describe Natasha Gordon. Ripe, earthy, soft, warm and unbelievably sexy... 'That you'd rather have a safe double bed?'

'Safe?' There was nothing safe or comfortable about this relationship. He had no idea what Natasha would say or do next. What he would do. His fingers seemed to burn when he touched her. He had no control over his responses... 'You will live to regret that.'

'Promises, promises...' For a moment they just looked at one another, then she turned away from the intensity of it and he allowed her to break the contact between them. 'Actually, robust is good. My family still treat me as if I've been stuck back together with some very dodgy glue and might fall apart at any moment.'

'No swimming, because pools are a germ factory and who knows what's in the sea?' he suggested.

'That's pretty much how it went.'

'It must have been difficult for them to truly believe that you've made a full recovery,' he said. 'I imagine you never quite trust the fates once you've been through something like that.'

'It wasn't just my parents. I've got three older brothers and they lived through it, too. Tom, the eldest, became a doctor because of what happened to me.'

'What about the other two?'

'James is a vet; Harry is a sports teacher. He's nearest in age to me and appointed himself my personal bodyguard when I started school. If anyone got too close, too rough, watch out.'

He knew he'd have been the same, but he could see it wouldn't be much fun to be on the receiving end of that kind of protection. 'How did you cope with that?'

'I regret to say that I loved it. I was a proper little princess,' she admitted ruefully, 'and, with three gorgeous brothers, everyone wanted to be my friend. It was only when I was fifteen and Harry discovered that I had a crush on a boy in the lower sixth that it all got out of hand.'

He grinned. 'I suppose he warned him off his little sister?'

'Oh, it was worse, far worse than that. The poor guy obviously didn't have a clue that he was the object of my desire. He always smiled at me in the corridor—probably because I *was* Harry's sister—and I'd just built up this huge fantasy. As you do...' He glanced at her and she rolled her eyes. 'Teenage girls.'

'An alien species,' he agreed. 'And?'

'And my sweet brother asked him, as a personal favour, to take me as his date to a school disco.'

'You're kidding?'

'I wish,' she said, 'but Harry was captain of sport and played under-eighteen rugby for the county. A request from him was in the nature of a decree from Mount Olympus.'

'So you had your dream date?'

'Bliss city.'

'But?'

She sighed. 'There is always a "but",' she agreed. 'I discovered what Harry had done, which was a total nightmare, but worse, much worse, I discovered that everyone else knew.'

'Before? After? During?'

'During. The classic overheard gossip in the loo... The girl he would have taken if Harry hadn't stuck his oar in was giving vent to her feelings about the spoiled, fat little cow who'd got her brother to twist her boyfriend's arm.'

'Ouch,' he said, flippantly enough, but deep down he was imagining what that must have been like for an over-protected fifteen-year-old girl. The embarrassment, the shame... 'What did you do?'

'I waited in the cubicle until they'd gone, then I slipped out of school and walked home.'

'Of course you did. How far was it?'

'A couple of miles. It wouldn't have been a problem, but I'd abandoned my coat because I didn't want anyone to see me leave.'

'Coat? What time of year was this?'

'It was the Christmas disco,' she said, and he let slip a word that he immediately apologised for.

'No, you're okay.' She held up her hand and began to count off the reasons why that word was just about perfect. First finger... 'There was the no-coat thing, which on any level was pretty dumb.' Second finger... 'There were the sparkly new shoes which weren't made for long-distance walking and fell apart after half a mile.' Third finger... 'Then it began to rain.'

'Your date didn't miss you?'

'Not for a while. When a girl disappears into a cloak-room who knows how long she'll be and I don't suppose he was in any hurry...' She shrugged. 'Anyway, my feet hurt, my dress was ruined and my life was over. Worse, I knew my parents would be waiting up for me, wanting to hear about my date. I couldn't face all that concern, all that sympathy, so I hid in the garden shed.'

'Oh, I can see where this is going. No one knew where you were. They organised a search party, called the police, dragged the river?'

'All of the above.'

'You're kidding?'

She laughed at his horrified reaction. 'Okay, not the river. Tom came looking for a torch and found me before it got that far. I was given a severe talking to by the local constabulary on the subject of responsibility and Dad grounded me for the whole of the Christmas holidays. No parties or holiday outings for me. Not much of a punishment, to be honest. I wanted to hibernate.'

'He knew that. He was making it easy for you.'

'Oh... Of course he was.' She shook her head. 'I never realised.'

'You were upset.'

'It got worse. School insisted that I had "counselling",' she said, making quote marks with her fingers, 'because obviously anyone who behaved so irrationally, so irresponsibly, had problems and needed help.'

Hardly irrational, he thought. More like a wounded animal going to ground. Something he knew all about.

'Not a Christmas to remember, I'm guessing.'

'White-faced parents, Harry in the doghouse with everyone. A total lack of ho-ho-ho. On the upside, by the time the holidays were over there were other scandals to talk about.'

'And the downside?'

'I'm still trying to prove that I can put one foot in front of the other without one of them holding my hand. Proving to my brothers that their broken little sister is all mended.'

Darius, thinking that if they'd seen her laying into him they might be convinced, said, 'Any luck?'

'The nearest I came was last Christmas when I drove home in the BMW.'

'Ho-ho-ho!'

She dug him in the ribs with her elbow. 'Men are so shallow. If I'd known how easy it was to impress them I'd have saved my bonuses for a flash car instead of putting down a deposit on my flat.'

'The fact that you didn't proves how smart you are.'

She sighed. 'Not smart enough to see this coming. Every morning I wake up and, just for a moment, everything is normal.'

Ten seconds, he thought. You had about ten seconds when you thought life still made sense before that jolt as you remembered and it was like the first moment all over again.

'I just feel so stupid.'

'Only someone you trust, someone you love can betray you, Natasha. It always comes out of left field.' He felt, rather than saw her turn to look at him. There would be a question mark rippling the creamy skin between her brows and he held his breath, waiting for the questions.

How did he know? When had his world come crashing down? Who had betrayed him? For what seemed an age the only sound was a blackbird perched high in the cedar tree. It was one of those long silences that the unwary rushed to fill and, even though he recognised the danger, he found himself tempted to tell her anyway.

She stirred before he could gather the words. Begin…

'The real downside was the guilt,' she said. 'I was old enough then to see what it did to my mother, to understand what she must have been through when I was little, so when Dad suggested I take my degree at Melchester University…'

Conflicting emotions twisted his gut. Relief that she'd let him off the hook, regret that he'd missed his chance.

'You wanted to make it up to them,' he said.

'It was okay, actually. Melchester has one of the best estate management courses in the country and, with all those lads living away from home for the first time, I was never short of a date.'

He doubted her mother's cooking was the only lure but he didn't want to think about that. 'So what made you toss away the dream job with the National Trust and run away to London to work for Miles Morgan?'

'I live in a small town. I was the little girl who'd had leukaemia. My sickness defined me. No one could see past it, not even my family.'

'So you finally made the break.'

'No... I lied to them, Darius.'

'Lied?'

'I knew that if I took the National Trust job, just down the road, I'd never leave. Never do anything. I'd marry someone I'd known all my life, who knew everything I'd ever done...'

'You told them you didn't get it?'

She nodded. 'It felt like breaking out of jail.' She tossed away the dregs of her coffee, staring out over the neglected lawn. 'I'll be honest. This isn't where I saw myself five years on from my degree, but I've worked harder than any-one so that I wouldn't have to go home and prove them all right.' She turned to look at him. 'You think I'm terrible, don't you? That I don't know how lucky I am to have a fam-ily who cares about me.'

Close. Very close. Apparently he wasn't the only one reading body language, studying inner depths. She must have learned a thing or two watching the men and women trying to hide their reactions to the houses she showed them, playing their cards close to their chest.

'I have no family,' he said, 'so I'm in no position to judge.'

'None?' And in a moment her expression turned from inward reproach to concern. 'I'm so sorry, Darius. That's really tough. What happened to your parents?'

Yes, well, that was the thing about trusting someone with your secrets; it was supposed to be a two-way deal but his moment of weakness had passed and he was already regretting this excursion into her past. Why complicate something as simple as sex?

'I have no parents.' He drained his coffee, screwed the top back on the flask and put it back in her bag. 'Did you ever tell them the truth?' he asked before she could push him for details. 'About the job?'

She shook her head.

'Maybe you should,' he advised. Clearly she was harbouring the guilt.

'They'd be devastated. And now, after all that horrible stuff in the paper, all those between-the-lines insinuations that I'm mentally unstable, they're out of their minds worried again.'

Her eyes were shining, but the tears were more of anger than anything else, he was certain. Was that how it was? Love? This complicated mishmash of guilt, anxiety, the desperate need not to hurt, to protect? Add in passion, sacrifice, the world well lost and you were well and truly stuffed... Or maybe blessed beyond measure.

Natasha blinked back the threatening tears and he put his arm around her, drew her close. There was a moment of stiffness, resistance and then she melted against him. 'My mother is desperate for me to go with them on the annual trek to Cornwall so that she can look after me,' she said. 'Heal me with sea air, walks on the beach, evening games of Scrabble.'

'Instead, you're playing hide the sausage in the woods with a disreputable sculptor who's going to put your naked body on display for the entire world to see,' he said.

She snorted, buried her face into his shoulder and suddenly, sitting there, his arm around her, both of them shaking with laughter, felt like a perfect moment.

Above them the swallows swooped just above head height, the scent of roses was drifting on a warm breeze and the temptation to stay there, looking out over the heat-hazed valley, almost overwhelmed him.

CHAPTER SEVEN

'DARIUS?'

He stirred and Natasha lifted her head, looked up at him. 'I'm sorry I shouted at you.'

'I'm not.' Tears of pain and laughter had clumped her eyelashes together. He used the pad of his thumb to wipe away one that had spilled over, kissed lips that were raised in what felt like an invitation. 'You can tell your family from me that they don't have a thing to worry about. You are strong in every way and I'm really glad you're on my side.'

Really glad as he kissed her again and, lost in the sweetness of her mouth, for once in his life not thinking about an exit strategy. It should be scaring the wits out of him, but the connection between them had an honesty that overrode any fear of commitment. Natasha needed him on her side to re-establish her career, didn't know that security guard from Adam and yet she had instantly empathised with him and she hadn't hesitated to give it to him with both barrels when she thought he was wrong. How many women in her situation would have done that?

When he was with her, he had no sense of losing himself, but of becoming something greater.

Blessed.

It was Natasha who moved.

'Enough of this maudlin self-pity,' she said. 'I've got work to do.'

He looked back at the house. Huge, empty... 'Are you going to be all right on your own?'

She gave him a warning look and he held up his hands. 'Sorry...'

'No... I shouldn't be so defensive.' Then, as he made a reluctant move, 'Actually, there is one thing.'

'Yes?'

Tash had felt the exact moment that Darius had wanted to move. For a blissful few minutes he'd been still, utterly relaxed and his kiss had been so tender that tears had once again threatened to overwhelm her.

After such an emotional exchange most men would have said *anything* but that shuttered 'yes' was warning enough, if she'd needed it, not to get too deeply involved with Darius Hadley. He wasn't a keeper and no one could protect her from that kind of pain.

'If I find any diaries, can I borrow them?'

'Diaries?'

'I imagine there are diaries, letters?' she prompted. 'Something interesting must have happened in three and a half centuries. You've got a ballroom, so presumably there were country balls? The occasional drama over a little inappropriate flirting? Maybe a duel?' she added, just to get a response.

'I have no idea,' he said stiffly, all his defences back up.

'Oh, for goodness' sake, Darius, lighten up,' she said crossly. 'If there had been any scandal to be dug up, the newspapers would have been all over it when that blasted ad became a news item.'

It didn't mean there wasn't a family skeleton rattling around in the cupboard because it was obvious that something wasn't right. He'd changed the subject faster than greased lightning when she'd asked him about his parents.

She lifted an eyebrow, inviting him to come clean, but even yesterday, with a bulge in his pants that had to have hurt, he'd been unreadable, hiding whatever he was thinking, feeling. What had it taken to build that mask?

What would it take, she wondered, to shatter it?

No, no, no…

'A house that grand, that old, must have hosted some interesting people over the centuries?' she persisted. It was all very well to casually toss out the words 'social media', but posting pictures of the house on Facebook and flinging 'buy this' Tweets around like confetti wasn't going to do the job.

'Not interesting in your sense of the word. The Hadleys were riding, shooting, fishing country squires with no pretensions to high society.'

'More Jane Austen than Georgette Heyer,' she said with a sigh. 'I don't suppose she ever came to tea? Jane Austen,' she added. Much as she loved Georgette Heyer's books, a visit from her wouldn't arouse the same kind of interest. 'I need a way in, something to grab the attention, create interest, start a buzz going.'

'Why don't you make up a story?'

'Excuse me?'

'Most family history is based on Chinese whispers— expanded and decorated with every retelling. Our story is that James Hadley was given the estate by Charles II for services rendered during his exile. How much more likely is it that he bought it cheap for a quick sale from one of Cromwell's confederates who, come the Restoration, decided the climate in the New World might be better for his health?'

'You're such a cynic, Darius Hadley.'

Off the dangerous territory of recent history, he grinned. 'A realist. Who's going to challenge you if you say Jane Austen stayed one wet week in April and, confined to the house, spun a story to keep everyone amused?'

'I have no doubt that some obsessive Janeite would know exactly where she was during that particular week.'

'Really?'

'I'm afraid so. They didn't have email or Skype or television to keep them amused so they wrote long detailed letters to their family and friends telling them where they were, what they were doing. And instead of blogging, they kept *diaries*...' She lifted her hands in a *ta-da* gesture.

'Being caught out in a blatant lie might grab the house another headline. *Mad Estate Agent Lies About Austen Connection*?' he offered. 'You did say any publicity would be good publicity.'

'I think you've had all that kind of "good" publicity you can handle and I'm trying to restore my reputation, not sink it without a trace so, unless you can point me to an entry in one your ancestors' diaries along the lines that "Mrs Austen visited with her daughters, Cassandra and Jane. It rained all week, but Jane kept the children amused acting out scenes from a little history of England she has written..." we'll save that as a last resort.'

'You're the expert,' he said. 'You'll find the diaries in my grandmother's room. She was writing a history of the house. I don't know if she ever finished it.'

'A history?' She was practically speechless. 'There's a history! For heaven's sake, Darius, talk about pulling hen's teeth!'

He grinned. 'I've made the woman happy. If there's nothing else?'

'No... Yes...' She fished in the picnic bag and produced a small plastic box. 'Take Gary these cookies from me. They're not as healthy as grapes, but they'll help a cup of hospital tea go down.'

Tash let herself into the house, dealt with the alarm and then, as the Land Rover rattled into life, she turned and watched it disappear as the drive dipped and curved through the woods. It seemed a little early for hospital visiting, but he'd shown no interest in going inside the house and she suspected that it served as a useful excuse to avoid whatever it was that he didn't want to talk about.

Despite her airy assurance that she would be fine, it was a huge old place, undoubtedly full of ghosts and, as she opened the glazed doors that led from the entrance lobby into the main reception hall, what struck her first was the stillness, the silence.

Out of the corner of her eye she saw something move, but when she swung round she realised that it was only her reflection in a dusty mirror.

Heart beating in her throat, she looked around but nothing stirred except the dust motes she'd set dancing in the sunlight pouring down from the lantern fifty feet above her and, just for a moment, she was back in the studio with Darius holding her, limp, sated in his arms. Reliving the desperate frustration when that wretched guard had turned up.

They were so not done.

No, no, no... Concentrate...

Beneath the mirror, an ornate clock on the hall table had long since stopped. Dead leaves had drifted into the corner of each tread of that dratted staircase. All it needed was a liveried footman asleep against the newel post and she would have stepped into the *Sleeping Beauty* picture book she'd had as a child.

As the germ of an idea began to form, she began to film the scene in front of her, panning slowly around the grand entrance hall with its shadowy portraits, an ormolu clock sitting on an elegant serpentine table thickly layered with dust, paused on the room reflected in soft focus through the hazy surface of the gilded mirror.

She opened doors to shuttered rooms where filtered light gave glimpses of ghostly furniture swathed in dust sheets, climbed the magnificent Tudor staircase—not a woodworm in sight—and explored bedrooms in varying stages of grandeur.

There was a four-poster bed that looked as if Queen Elizabeth I might have slept in it in the master suite. Next door was a suite for the mistress of the house—a comfortable, less daunting bedroom, a dressing room and bathroom and a small sitting room with a chaise longue, a writing desk and a bookshelf filled with leather-bound journals. Research material for his grandmother's history.

The desk had just one wide drawer and nestling inside it was a heavy card folder tied together with black ribbon and bearing the title *A History of Hadley Chase by Emma Hadley.* She had just untied the ribbon and laid back the cover to reveal a drawing of the Tudor house that had been added to and 'improved' over the years when her phone pinged, warning her of an incoming text.

It was from Darius.

Darius stopped twenty yards from the main gate and the gatehouse cottage that Gary shared with his grandmother.

Mary Webb had been his grandmother's cook and the nearest thing to a mother he'd ever had. She'd given him the spoons to lick when she was making cakes, stuck on the plasters when he'd scraped a knee, given him a hug when his dog died. And, like everyone else in this place, had known his history and kept it from him.

When he'd learned the truth he'd walked away from the house and everyone connected with it and never looked back. That had been his choice, but while he had a home, a career, there was no guarantee that Gary, a few years older, who'd made him a catapult, lain in the dark with him watching for badgers, taught him to ride a motorbike, would have either when the estate was sold.

This is my land...

The words had come so easily. But they were hollow without the responsibilities that went with it. *Noblesse oblige.* Natasha hadn't used those words, but when she'd rounded on him that was the subtext.

She'd asked him how long it had been since he'd set foot on this estate. Almost as long as he'd lived here. An age. A lifetime. He would never have come back if he'd had his way and yet, because of her, he was here. Not for the land, but for a woman. The irony was not lost on him.

He took out his phone, sent her a two-word text and when he looked up Mary Webb was standing on the doorstep. Seventeen years older and so much smaller than he remembered.

Sixteen years.

The text was unsigned, but it came from Darius and could only mean one thing. She'd asked him how long it was since he'd last set foot on Hadley Chase. He hadn't answered, but he had been listening.

Sixteen years...

The article she'd read about his commission for the sculpture of the horse had mentioned that he'd been at the Royal College of Art and from the date she'd been able to work out that he had to be thirty-one, maybe thirty-two. That meant he'd have been sixteen or seventeen when he left the Chase, long before his grandfather became sick or he'd left for art school. It suggested a family row of epic proportions. A breach that had never been healed. Scarcely any wonder he hadn't wanted her digging around, poking in the corners stirring up ghosts.

But this was a tiny crack and through it other questions flooded in. Not just what had caused the rift, but where could a hurting teenage boy with no family have gone?

She tried to imagine herself in that situation. Imagine

that instead of hiding out in the shed, she'd run away. It
happened every day. Teenagers running away from situa-
tions they couldn't handle.

Where would she have run to? How would she have
lived?

How would she have felt returning home after sixteen
years, a stranger, changed beyond recognition from the cos-
setted girl who'd painted her nails, pinned up her hair, put
on a new dress and sparkly shoes to go to a school disco?

He'd shown no interest, no emotional attachment to the
property until that security guard had ordered him to leave
but then the claim had been instinctive. Possessive.

'This is my land...'

She looked around her. Darius had lived here while he
was growing up, going to school. All his formative years
had been spent roaming the estate. In this house. It had
made him who he was, given him the strength to survive
on his own. She would have expected a photograph on the
desk, on the bedside table. There was nothing, but there
had to be traces of him here. His room...

When she'd visited the Chase in order to prepare the
details for the kind of glossy sales brochure a house of
this importance demanded, there had been a team of them
from Morgan and Black, walking the land, detailing the
outbuildings, the cottages, the boathouse. Inside, she had
concentrated on the main reception and bedrooms while
junior staff had gone through the minor rooms, the attics.

She arranged the desk to look as if the writer had just left
it for a moment, took photographs of that and the view from
the window, then picked up the folder and went in search
of the room which had been Darius Hadley's private space.

She found it at the far end of the first floor corridor.
Grander than most bedrooms, with a high ceiling, tall win-
dows looking out over the park and furnished with pieces
that had obviously been in the house for centuries. And yet

it was still recognisable for what it was. A boy's bedroom. Unchanged since he'd abandoned it.

Her brother Tom was about the same age and he'd had the same poster above his bed, the same books on his shelves.

The similarity ended with the books and posters. Tom had always known what he wanted to do and by the time he was seventeen he'd had a skeleton in his room, medical diagrams on the walls.

Darius, too, had been focused on the future. There were wall-to-wall drawings, tacked up with pins, curling at the edges.

One of them, the drawing of a laughing retriever, each curl of his coat, each feather of his tail so full of life that he looked as if he was about to bound off the paper after a rabbit.

On a worktable lay a folder filled with watercolours. Distant views of the house, the hills, the birds and animals that roamed the estate. The faint scent of linseed oil still clung to an easel leaning against a far wall. She opened a wooden box stacked beside it. Brushes, dried up tubes of paint. He'd moved on from sketches and watercolours to oil, but none of those were here.

She turned to the wardrobe and a lump formed in her throat as she saw his clothes. A pair of riding boots, walking shoes, battered old trainers bearing the shape of his youthful foot lined up beneath shirts, a school uniform, jackets, a suit and, in a suit bag from a Savile Row tailor, what must have been his first tux, never worn.

What kind of a life had he had here? Privileged, without a doubt, and yet he'd apparently walked away from it, leaving everything behind. His clothes, his art, his life.

She'd been seven or eight when Tom was that age and he'd seemed like a god to her then, but when she'd been sixteen, seventeen, the boys in her year had seemed so im-

mature, so useless. She couldn't imagine any of them cop-
ing without their mother to do their washing, put food in
front of them, provide a taxi service.

She sat on the narrow bed, rubbed her hand over the
old Welsh quilt that he'd slept under, then kicked off her
shoes, leaned back against an impressive headboard, putting herself in his place, looking out of the window at the
view he'd grown up with, trying to imagine what had been
so bad that it had driven him away. And failing. It was so
beautiful here, so tranquil.

She sighed. No doubt her home life would have looked
enviable to an outsider and in many ways it was. But she'd
been older, an adult when she'd left. He'd been a boy.

She let it go and, propping the folder against her thighs,
began to read his grandmother's history of Hadley Chase.

Darius was right—nothing important had happened,
no one of great significance was mentioned—and yet his
grandmother had edited the journals, adding her own com-
mentary and illustrations on events, providing an insight
into the lives of those living and working in the house, on
the estate and in the village since the seventeenth century.
The births, marriages, deaths. The celebrations. The trag-
edies, changes that affected them all. Tash had reached the
late eighteenth century when her phone rang.

'Hi...' she said, hunting for a tissue.

Darius, pacing Mary's living room while she packed a
bag, heard the kind of sniff that only went with tears.

'Natasha? What's happened? Are you hurt?'

'No...' Another sniff. 'It's nothing.'

'You're crying.'

'I was just reading about an outbreak of smallpox in
the village in 1793. Seven children died, Darius. One of
them was the three-year-old son of Joshua Hadley. He wrote
about him, about the funeral. It's heartbreaking...'

She'd found the history. It had figured heavily in his

education as the heir to the estate and the death of small children had been a fact of life before antibiotics.

'It was over two hundred years ago,' he reminded her.

'I know. I'm totally pathetic, but your grandmother drew a picture of his grave. It's so small. This isn't just a history; it's a work of art.'

'And full of smallpox, floods, crop failure.'

'Full of the lives of the people who've lived here. Not just the bad bits, but the joys, the celebrations. Your grandmother's illustrations are exquisite. Clearly it's in the genes,' she prompted.

He ignored the invitation to talk about his grandmother. 'You'll find Joshua's portrait in the dining room.'

'Actually, I'm looking at some of your early work right now,' she said, not giving up. 'Watercolours.'

'Chocolate-box stuff,' he said dismissively.

'That's a bit harsh. I love the drawing of your dog. What was his name?'

What was it about this woman? Every time he spoke to her, she churned up memories he'd spent years trying to wipe out. The only reason he was even here, being dragged back into the past, was because of her.

He should have just signed the whole lot over to the Revenue and let it go. It wasn't too late... Except there were things he had to do. People he had to protect.

'Darius?'

'Flynn,' he said. 'His name was Flynn.'

'He looks real enough to stroke.'

Even now, all these years later, he could feel the springy curls beneath his fingers. Smell the warm dog scent. Leaving him behind had been the hardest thing, but he'd been old—too old to leave the certainty of a warm hearth and a good dinner.

He'd mocked her sentimentality over a child who'd died

two hundred years ago but now he was the one with tears stinging at the back of his eyes.

'Darius, are you okay?'

He cleared his throat. 'Yes…'

'So, can I use all this stuff?'

'Will a smallpox outbreak help to the sell the house, do you think?' he asked.

'I'll probably miss out that bit.'

'Good decision.'

'So that's yes?'

'That's a yes with all the usual conditions.'

'You've already got me naked,' she reminded him.

He'd meant the ones about keeping his name out of it but, just as easily as she could dredge up the sentimental wasteland buried deep in his psyche, she could turn him on, make him laugh. 'You're naked?' he asked.

'Give me thirty seconds.'

He gripped the phone a little tighter. The temptation was there, but the thought of walking back into that house was like a finger of ice driving into him. 'Not even thirty minutes, I'm afraid. I've hit a complication.'

'Where are you?' she asked, as quick to read a shift in tone as body language.

'I stopped at the gatehouse to visit Mary Webb, Gary's grandmother,' he explained. 'He lives with her.'

'Oh… That was kind.'

'It was a duty call. She used to be my grandparents' cook. I couldn't just drive past.' He'd thought he could. He'd spent the last seventeen years mentally driving past.

'Kindness, duty, it doesn't matter, Darius, as long as you do it.'

'I'm glad you think so. She's five-foot-nothing and frail as a bird these days but it hasn't stopped her from reading me the riot act.'

'Give her a cookie,' she said, not asking why she was

angry. No doubt she understood how a woman would feel who'd lost—been abandoned by—a child she'd cared for, loved since infancy. Who, as a result of what happened that day, had lost her own grandson. His grandfather had not been a man to cross... 'People from the village are keeping an eye on her, doing her shopping, but she needs more than that so I'm taking her to see Gary, then driving her down to stay with her daughter in Brighton.'

'That should be a fun drive.'

'I'll blame you every mile of the way.'

'If it helps,' she said.

No, but thinking about her might. 'I'll survive,' he assured her. Probably. 'But I have no idea how long I'll be.'

'Don't worry about it. You take care of Mrs Webb. I can sort out some transport for myself. There's a bus to Swindon and I can catch a train from there. Don't give it a second thought. It's not a problem. Piece of cake—'

Her mouth was running away with her as she tried to hide her disappointment. It should have been an ego boost but all he wanted was to reach down the phone and hold her. Helpless, he waited until she began to repeat herself, finally ground to a halt, before he said, 'I'm taking her in Gary's car. I'll leave the Landie keys under a flowerpot in the porch for you.'

'Oh.'

'That's it?' he asked. 'You're finally lost for words?'

'No. I was just thinking that if you're bringing Gary's car back, I might as well stay here and wait for you.'

'It'll be late.'

'We might have to stay the night,' she agreed.

Not in a million years... 'I've got a better idea. Let's meet halfway at your place. We can have that picnic you promised me.'

'Oh? And what will you bring to the party?'

'A bottle of something chilled and a packet of three?' he offered.

'Three? That's a bit ambitious, isn't it?'

'One for yesterday, one for this morning, one for fun?' he suggested.

Her laugh was rich and warm. 'Talk, talk, talk…' she said, and ended the call.

He was grinning when he looked up and saw Mary watching him.

'My suitcase is on the bed,' she said primly. Then, as he passed her, she put her hand on his arm. 'It was the motorbike, Darius. That's why he told you about your Dad. Gary never cared about any of the other stuff you had, but that motorbike…'

'I know…'

It was Gary, with a battered old machine that he was renovating, who'd taught him to ride on the estate roads, so when he'd come down and found a brand-new silver motorbike waiting for him on his seventeenth birthday, the first thing he'd done was fire it up and drive it down to show him.

Cock-of-the-walk full of himself, too immature to understand how the one who'd always been the leader might feel when he saw him astride a machine so far out of his own reach. The understanding, in that split second, of the reality of their friendship; how, from that moment on, every step would take them further apart. For him there would be sixth form, university, the eventual ownership of this estate. For Gary, who'd left school at sixteen with no qualifications, there would be only a life of manual labour on little more than the minimum wage. And he'd used the only weapon he had to put himself back on top.

'He didn't do anything wrong. He told the truth, what he knew of it, that's all.'

'He was a stiff, proud man, your grandfather. He broke

your grandmother's heart, barring your father from the house while he stayed with your mother. The poor lady was never the same after. It wasn't that she didn't want to love you, Darius, just that she'd lost so much that she couldn't bear the risk.'

'Everyone lost, Mary. My grandfather most of all.'

Tash rolled off his bed and crossed to the window to look out across the park in the direction of the gates, rubbing her arms briskly to rid herself of the tingle of excitement that, just hearing the sound of his voice, riffled her skin into goose bumps.

Silly. She couldn't see the gatehouse cottage for the trees, but she was still grinning. She'd taken their relationship a step beyond a place Darius was comfortable with, hoping it would help him open up. Maybe it had. He'd stopped to talk to Gary's grandmother and the fact that she was angry with him suggested a strong emotional bond.

You only got angry with people you cared about. The fact that he'd mentioned it suggested that it mattered; he hadn't just called in, done the minimum, but had seen a need and acted on it. The journey might not be a comfortable one, but she doubted it would be silent; Mary Webb knew his secrets and he would be able to talk to her.

The fact that he'd felt able to tell her that she'd been angry suggested...

Stop it. Right there. The last thing she needed right now was a load of emotional complications messing with her head. Keep it simple.

Darius pressed the bell and Natasha's voice, distorted by static, said, 'Who's there?'

'You'd better not be expecting anyone else.'

'My cake is in great demand,' she said.

'Sugarlips!'

'First floor, the door on the right,' she said, and buzzed him up.

'I'm in the kitchen,' she called as he opened the door, and he kicked off his shoes alongside hers and followed her voice.

Her top, something silky in a rich chocolate, slid from her shoulder, a short pink skirt in some floaty material rose up, drawing attention to her long legs, bare feet, as she reached for a couple of wine glasses and, without saying a word, he put his arms around her and buried his mouth in the delicious curve between her shoulder and neck, sucking in her flesh, nipping at the sweet spot at the base of her neck.

A shiver of pleasure went through her as his hands found her breasts and she relaxed into him. It was the thought of this moment that had sustained him through an emotionally fraught day. The thought of holding her, breathing in the scent of her hair, her skin...

'Hello, you,' she said, laughing as she turned in his arms, reaching up to put her arms around his neck. Her hands didn't quite make it, her smile fading as her eyes searched his face and instead she cradled his cheeks in her palms, her thumbs wiping the hollows beneath his eyes as if to brush away dark shadows that only she could see. 'You've had a rough day...'

'No talking,' he said roughly. His ears were ringing with sixteen years of history as they'd talked about about everything, about every*one* but his mother. And now when Natasha would have answered him he cut her off with an abrupt, hungry kiss. For a heartbeat she was shocked into stillness and then she wrapped her arms around his neck, one of those long legs against his thigh and melted against him, her hot silk mouth the entrance to paradise.

He kissed her slow and deep while his hands reacquainted themselves with the feel of her skin, the already familiar shape of her curves, spreading wide around her waist, pushing up her top as his thumbs caressed the hollows of her stomach, his fingers teasing out all the little hotspots in her ribs.

Her fingers tangled in his hair, hanging on to him as she responded with little moans against his tongue and he fed on her sweet, spicy nectar that blotted out memory, blotted out everything but this moment, this need.

She uttered a soft cry as he broke off to get rid of her top, her bra and then leaned back with a sigh of contentment as he took his mouth, his tongue on a slow exploration of her body.

Definitely no talking...

CHAPTER EIGHT

TASH WAS INCAPABLE of coherent speech as Darius, his hands cradling her backside, sucked on the sensitive spot beneath her chin, curled his tongue around the horseshoe bone at the base of her throat, trailed hot, moist kisses between her breasts.

She whimpered as he ignored them and kept on going down, down, then he hit her navel and his tongue did things that had her gasping, breathless, climbing up him with her legs.

He propped her on the counter without missing a beat, then, with his hands free, he pushed up her skirt and slid his hand beneath the scrap of lace, pressing his thumb against the hot, swollen little button screaming for attention, then slowly circled it, in time with his tongue.

'Unngh…' she said, grabbing the collar of his polo shirt and hauling it, hand over hand, until it was over his head, then swallowed as she got the full impact of his powerful shoulders, arms moulded by the heaving of tons of clay, stone, metal, his broad chest arrowing to a narrow waist, hips, a mouth-watering bulge…

'Want to do it here?' he asked, his eyes burnished coal, teasing her with the tip of his finger before plunging it deep inside her.

'Unngh uuuunngh,' she urged, tightening around it, wanting more, wanting everything.

'Or would you rather move this to a nice safe bed?'

Safe...

There was nothing safe about this except the leaving-nothing-to-chance protection she'd stowed in the tiny seam pocket of her skirt and she answered him by taking it out, holding it between her teeth as, never taking her eyes from his, she tugged on his belt, flipped the button...

She looked up and, taking the condom from between her lips, he lowered his mouth to within a breath of hers and said, 'Don't stop now.'

He closed the gap, taking the word 'kiss' to a whole new meaning as, fingers shaking, she lowered his zip with the utmost care, eased her hands inside his jeans and pushed them down, releasing him. Clung to his hips as he disposed of her underwear, sheathed himself.

Then he looked up, straight into her eyes. 'Ready?' he asked.

'No talking,' she whispered and he was inside her with a thrust that went to her toes, held it while she caught her breath, opened her eyes. 'Don't stop now,' she murmured, wrapping her arms around his neck, her legs around his waist, taking in everything he had to give.

He gave it slowly, totally focused on her, reading her response to every thrust, every touch, taking this most basic of all acts and, instead of snatching for swift satisfaction, raising it into something new, something extraordinary, only taking his own release when he'd brought her to the point of incoherent howling meltdown.

Tash, shaking, shattered, wasn't sure which of them was supporting the other, only that they were holding each other, her cheek pressed into the hollow of his shoulder, listening to his heart return to a slow steady thud, breathing in the arousing scent of fresh sweat. All she knew was that she was glad she'd shut the kitchen window. That it was double-glazed...

* * *

Darius was the first to recover, straightening, lifting Natasha to the floor, holding her until he was certain that she could support herself. Or maybe holding on to her so that she could support him.

That was so not how it was meant to be.

Wound up by a day that had been filled with memories he'd spent half a lifetime trying to eradicate, he'd come looking for a hot, fast, cleansing release. Basic sex. What had just happened was something else...

He cleared his throat. 'I don't know about you, but I could do with a drink.'

She lifted her head, kissed his cheek. 'Sounds perfect.' She spotted the bottle he'd put on the kitchen table, picked up the glasses and handed them to him. 'Bring them through to the bathroom.'

There was no way they could both cram into her tiny shower cubicle so Tash filled the tub, added some bubbles, lit scented candles. He brought two glasses half filled with a pale chilled wine, set the bottle on the ledge and climbed in. She settled between his legs, leaning back against his chest, sipping the wine in restful silence as she relived each moment, each touch.

So much for the keep-it-simple sex. That had been as far removed from the simple gratification of a basic need as she'd ever experienced. No one had ever concentrated so completely on her in that way. Given so much...

His skin, golden in the candlelight, was too tempting and she turned her head, found the tender spot behind his knee with her tongue. He rescued her glass as, spurred on by his instant reaction, she half turned to take her mouth on an exploration of the smooth silk of his inner thigh, then turned to face him.

'Here or in a nice safe bed?' she asked.

'No bed is ever going to be safe with you in it but I'll

risk it,' he said, drawing her up his body so that he could kiss her. 'And this time I'm going to lie back and let you do all the work.'

Not work... All pleasure.

Tash woke to the early-morning sun, her body all delicious aches, and the night came flooding back. How she had made him the centre of their lovemaking, focusing on him so intently that she could read his response to every touch, giving herself in a way that she had never imagined and discovering a whole new level of pleasure in doing so.

She turned to reach for him but she was alone but for a sheet a paper on the pillow beside her. He'd drawn her as she'd slept—her breasts exposed, the curve of her buttock visible above the sheet tangled around her thighs, her hand extended towards him as if calling him back to bed.

Anyone looking at it would know that she had spent the night making love to the artist. If it had been anyone else, she'd have said that it was beautiful, but looking at herself, so vulnerable, so exposed, was disturbing. And why had he left it? Did he leave a picture for all his lovers? Something for the scrapbook? Something to scandalise the grandchildren?

Coffee. She needed coffee. Peeling herself off the bed, she tucked the drawing away in a drawer, pulled on a wrap and went through to the kitchen.

There was a note propped up against the kettle.

Sorry to kiss and run, but the horse is booked in at the foundry next week. Keep the Land Rover and the house keys for as long as you need them. D.

Next week? The horse had looked a long way from finished when she'd seen it and yet he'd taken a precious day to drive her to Hadley Chase. Of course this was a Darius

Hadley sculpture. What she thought was finished and what he considered finished…

She reached for her phone to text him…what? Thanks for the keys? For his time? For everything? There had been a lot of 'everything' to thank him for.

Keep it simple, she reminded herself, keying in the words:

Thanks for yesterday. N.

That covered it. Then she realised that she'd used N instead of T, which made it a lot more complicated. He was not a keeper and she was Tash, not Natasha. This was no more than a bit of a fling while she sorted herself out, she reminded herself.

So why did it feel like so much more?

Because she was all over the place. Because her life had been turned upside down. Because he was so much more…

She hit send before her brain fried tying itself in knots avoiding the truth.

Tash spent the next few days building up a media presence for Hadley Chase. She scanned some of the watercolours and used one that Darius had painted of the house as the header for the Facebook page, the ready-made web page she'd invested in and the Twitter account. It was very similar to the photograph she'd taken. No wonder he'd said she had a good eye.

Once it was all in place, she scheduled one-hundred-and-forty-character 'bites' from the history on the Twitter feed, adding his grandmother's exquisite illustrations, and then she did the same thing with the rest of his paintings. She linked it to the Facebook page and to the webpage where she'd laid out the house details.

She recorded a voice-over for the 'Sleeping Beauty'

video that she'd made inside the house and posted that on YouTube, linking each room to something from the history.

By the following week, she was gathering quite a following, getting lots of shares and re-Tweets, but most of the people who commented were less interested in the house than the artist and the history.

Who had painted the watercolours? Where could they buy them? Were prints available? Was the house open to the public? Where could they buy the book?

So far, no one had connected the paintings with Darius Hadley—hardly surprising considering the sculptures that had made his name. She considered sending a link to the Facebook page to Freddie Glover. She knew he'd get it, and no doubt wet himself in his rush to get his hands on the pictures. But Darius had dismissed the pictures as chocolate-box stuff and, besides, she'd given him her word.

There was no word from Darius—well, he was busy—but whenever the doorbell rang she rushed to see who it was.

'Tash?'

'Hi, Mum,' she said, buzzing her up, quashing her disappointment as she reached for the kettle. 'This is a surprise. I thought you'd be busy cooking and packing for the holiday.'

'Cooking,' she said, taking a casserole dish from a basket and popping it into the fridge. 'I ran out of room in the freezer.'

As you do...

'And you came all the way to London to give it to me?' she teased.

'Not just that. I thought, since you aren't working, we could spend the day together. We could go shopping... maybe have afternoon tea at Claibournes? Dad offered to treat us.'

Oh, right. This wasn't just food, it was the entire take-your-mind-off-it scenario.

'Actually, Mum, I'm a bit busy.'

'You're working? Has Miles Morgan—?'

'No. I'm handling a private sale for a client,' she said quickly, ignoring the fact that the definition of a client was someone who paid for your services. After all, a first casting Darius Hadley bronze would be worth a bob or two. Assuming he was still interested. 'So, what are you shopping for? You've left it a bit late for holiday stuff.' And her mother never left anything until the last minute. Obviously, she'd decided on a little face-to-face persuasion to join them.

'The holiday is off.'

'Off?'

Her mother sighed, laid out a couple of cups and saucers, heated the teapot. 'We had a call last night. Apparently the water tank overflowed, a ceiling came down and the cottage is uninhabitable for the foreseeable future. The kids are devastated.'

'Oh…I'm sorry.'

She cracked a wry smile. 'Really?'

'Absolutely. I know how much you enjoy it.' It might not be her idea of a good time, but Cornwall was a spring half-term tradition that went way back, rain or shine, and as a child she'd loved it. When she had children of her own she would love it again. 'Can't you find somewhere else?'

'For nine adults and seven children at half-term? And it's the bank holiday.'

'Eight adults,' Tash reminded her, getting down the cake tin. 'Lemon drizzle?' she offered, putting it on a plate. 'What will you do?'

'Organise some day trips, I suppose. We'll manage.' She took a piece of cake, rolled her eyes in appreciation. 'You could open a cake shop,' she said. 'Or maybe an Internet home delivery service? Lots of demand for good home-made cake.'

'I could, but I won't.'

'Just a thought. Tell me about this private sale.'

'Actually, it's Hadley Chase.'

Her mother frowned. 'Isn't that the house—?'

'Yes. I've promised the owner that I'll find him a buyer.'

'And he agreed?'

'Why wouldn't he? I have a terrific track record.'

'With an agency behind you,' she said. 'Glossy bro-chures, ads in the *Country Chronicle*...' She stopped, real-ising that wasn't the most tactful thing to say. 'Advertising costs the earth.'

'Not necessarily.'

She showed her mother the Facebook page and got an unimpressed *humph*. 'People who buy stately homes aren't going to see this,' she said.

'It's all about getting a buzz going. Getting noticed by the media.' Getting them to follow you was the hardest part. They apparently took the view that they were there to be followed.

Her mother took another look. 'Well, you do seem to have a lot of comments.'

'Most of them asking who painted the picture of the house.' The one thing she couldn't tell anyone. 'Or if the history has been published and where can they buy it.' Maybe she should be following publishers. Art dealers.

'It is a lovely picture. Who did paint it?'

Yes, well, there was the rub.

'I found it in the house. It wasn't signed.'

'Well, someone who lived there was very talented.' She took another forkful of cake, then said, 'What you need is a plan.'

'This is the plan,' she admitted. 'Well, one of them. I've made a sort of *Sleeping Beauty* story. Pictures of the stairs covered in leaves, furniture shrouded in dust sheets, cob-webby attics, glimpses of the view through dusty windows, matching the room with sound bites from the history, and put it on YouTube.' She played it through.

'It's very…atmospheric.'

'Thanks. That's exactly what I was going for,' she said.

Her mother sighed. 'This is all very arty and interesting but what would you have done if Miles Morgan hadn't…' She made a vague gesture, clearly not wanting to say the words. 'To recover the situation?'

'Well, I would have suggested…' She stopped. Keep it simple… Okay, she couldn't afford to hire a firm of contract cleaners but maybe, just maybe… 'Mum, can I offer you a proposition?'

'You can offer me another piece of that cake,' she said, pouring out the tea, adding a splash of milk. 'What kind of proposition?'

'Well, you can see for yourself that Hadley Chase is a beautiful country house set in amazing grounds. It has a chalk stream with trout fishing for Dad and the boys, rods included,' she added. She'd seen them hung on racks in one of the storerooms. 'There are views to die for, and Hadley is a classic English village with thatched cottages, a centuries-old pub and a village green. I know it's not Cornwall,' she said quickly, 'but it will be free.'

'Well, that sounds delightful and incredibly generous of you, considering it's not your house,' her mother replied, suspicious rather than enthusiastic, 'but you seem to have glossed over the delightfully atmospheric cobwebs. And didn't it say in the paper that the staircase was about to fall down?'

'There is nothing wrong with the staircase that a vacuum, a duster and a little elbow grease won't fix.' She waited for the penny to drop. It didn't take long.

'So when you say "free", what you actually mean is that we'll be spending our holiday dealing with the dust and the leaves and whatever else is lingering in the corners. In other words, giving the place a thorough scrub?'

'Not all of it,' she protested. 'Just the main rooms.'

'And the bedrooms, unless we're going to camp on the lawn. And the bathrooms. And the kitchen.'

'I'll do the kitchen before you get there. Really, it's not that bad.'

Her mother sipped her tea.

'Seven days, eight adults,' she prompted. 'All I'm asking is an hour a day from each of you and in return you get to stay in an ancient and historic manor house. I promise,' she continued before her mother could raise any other objections, 'that no one at the WI will have holiday pictures to beat yours. Not some pokey little cottage, not even an apartment in a stately home, but the whole place, four-poster beds and a ballroom included, to yourselves.'

'I don't know, Tash—'

'You should read Emma Hadley's history. I've scanned it and printed it so you can take a copy with you. The illustrations are beautiful,' she said. 'You could give a talk. I'll make a PowerPoint presentation for you.' A tiny giveaway muscle in the corner of her mother's mouth twitched and, confident that she was hooked, Tash sat back. 'Of course, if it's too much for you, I could give Harry a call. If he and Lily have got nowhere booked for half-term I'm sure he would love to help...'

'You will be staying with us?' her mother asked, matching her guilt play and trumping it. 'Not just cleaning up the kitchen and then running away back to London?'

That was the thing with mothers. They could see through you, right down to the bone. A bit like a sculptor she knew...

'Oh, I'll have to be there,' she said. 'I'll be holding an open day on the last Saturday. With afternoon tea. Is there any chance of a few of your scones?'

'Is there any chance that you will be coming to Cornwall next year?'

She was a mere amateur compared to her mother.

'You can count on it. I've decided to take up surfing.'

Her mother, ignoring that, stood up. 'I suppose I'd better go home and get everyone organised. We'll bring our own bedding. And towels,' she added. 'Mice will almost certainly have made nests in the linen cupboards.'

Oh, joy…

'I'll ask one of the boys to pick you up on Saturday morning.'

'No need. Darius…Mr Hadley has loaned me his Land Rover.'

'*Darius* Hadley?' Her mother frowned. 'That name rings a bell. Would I have seen him in *Celebrity*?'

'I couldn't say,' she said truthfully.

Tash still had the keys and she had Darius's permission to do whatever it took to sell the house. No need to disturb him when he was so busy. Except, of course, someone would have to inform the security people that he would be having house guests.

And an open day on the Saturday.

What should she do? Text, phone and leave a message or go and see him? Her mother would not be amused if the police arrived mob-handed to evict them. She had to be sure he'd got the message and if he was working flat-out he might not check his phone.

She would just have to go and see him.

It was quicker to take the Underground than drive across London or take the bus and, since there was a truck completely blocking his street, she'd clearly made the right decision.

There was quite a crowd watching the drama and she spotted Patsy among them. 'What's going on?'

'They're loading up the horse. Darius!' she called. 'You've got company.'

He appeared from behind the truck, sweaty, dusty. There was clay in his hair and smeared across his cheek where he'd wiped away sweat with the back of his hand and a week's worth of beard only added to the piratical look.

'Hang on,' he said, 'I just need to see this on its way.'

'Take your time.'

His face split in a wide grin. 'I always do.'

Oh, yes…

She caught Patsy's eye and hoped she hadn't said that out loud. Judging by the eye-roll, she didn't need to. 'Have you sold the house yet?' she asked.

'No, but I'm working on it.'

'If there's anything I can do—' she produced a business card '—give me a call.'

'I can't afford help,' she said. 'That's why I'm here. I've offered my family a week in the country in return for their help cleaning the place up.'

'Well, now, I can't afford to take my boy away this half-term. If you need more hands, I'll work for board and country air.'

'Well, thanks. The more the merrier.'

'Clear it with Darius and give me a ring,' she said, glancing at her watch. 'See you later.'

Tash pressed herself against the wall as the truck started up and Darius joined her as it slowly pulled away, the crated horse lashed down in the back. They watched it pull out into the main road and disappear, then he looked down at her.

'You look like ice cream. I'd kiss you,' he said, 'but I stink.'

'It's a good stink.' Earthy clay, freshly sawn pine mingled with the sharp scent of honest sweat and, lifting a hand to his face, she rubbed her palm against his beard. 'And I want to try this.'

He lifted her hand, touched it to his lips. 'That's all I've got,' he said, tucking her arm around his waist and, with his arm around her shoulder, headed up the street. 'I haven't been to bed since I got out of yours.'

She stopped. 'You took time out to take me to Hadley Chase when you were that pushed?'

'Don't...' He touched the space between her brows. 'Don't frown. I was already struggling. The house, a whole lot of mess being dragged up from the past... You fired me up.' He unlocked the door to a small mews cottage at the end of the street. 'How do you feel about being my muse?'

His muse? For just a moment the image of herself as his inspiration sparkled in her imagination. She forced herself back to earth. 'It sounds a bit Pre-Raphaelite to me. I'm getting images of scantily dressed women lounging around a cold and draughty studio while louche men discuss their vision. I think I'll pass.'

'I didn't say becoming my muse, I said being her.'

'I don't get a choice?'

'Neither of us do, apparently.'

'Oh... Well, I'm glad to have helped,' she said, leaning against him briefly. 'Have you eaten?'

'Patsy kept me fuelled up. Have you been trying to get hold of me?' he asked, taking a phone out of his back pocket. 'The battery on this is flatter than a pancake.'

'I did leave a message, but I thought if you were working you wouldn't pick it up.'

'It's that important?'

'I haven't sold the house,' she said quickly, 'but it was too important to leave to chance.'

'Scrub my back and you'll have my full attention,' he assured her, kicking off his boots in the tiny lobby, peeling off his T-shirt and letting it lie where it fell.

On the outside, the cottage fitted with the rest of the

street. Inside, it was bare polished wood floors, white walls, spare steel lamp fittings and old rubbed leather chairs.

He slipped the buckle of his belt, let his jeans fall, stepped out of them and, naked, walked up the open stair-case that led to a sleeping loft, not stopping until he reached a granite and steel wet room.

'If you're going to scrub my back you'd better lose the clothes or they'll get soaked,' he warned as he flipped the tap. His eyes gleamed wickedly. 'Or you could leave them on. Either way works for me.'

'Behave yourself.' She hadn't come dressed down. She'd wanted to make an impact, wanted him to notice her and even before she reached for the hem of the clinging cross-over top she was wearing she could see that she had. 'I have to go home on the Tube.'

She unhooked the swirl of printed chiffon that stopped six inches above her knee, kicked it away and stepped out of her shoes.

'Stop right there,' he said when she was down to the champagne lace bra and panties that she'd bought with birthday money and even in the sale had cost twice any-thing else she wore next to her skin. 'I really want to see those wet.'

'When you can do more than kiss my hand,' she said, but took her time over removing them since he appeared to like them so much. 'Turn round.'

His eyes were focused on her breasts. 'Do I have to?'

Oh, boy. That was a tough one. His thick dark curls, the streaks of clay on his cheeks, his chest, water sluicing over his skin gave him the elemental look of some tribal chief-tain who'd battled the elements and won through.

Every primitive instinct was urging her to take a step forward, press her body against his and go for it but the dark hollows in his temples, beneath his eyes warned her that it was the last thing he needed.

She picked a gel off the shelf, made a circular gesture with her finger and after a moment he turned, placed his hands flat against the granite, bracing himself, or more likely propping himself up.

His finely muscled back, narrow waist, taut buttocks were, if anything, even more distracting.

Get a grip, Tash. You can do this…

She applied the gel to his hair, stretching up on her toes to ease out the dried-in clay with her fingers, leaning into him to massage his scalp—her body, breasts sliding against him as the soap cascaded down his back.

He groaned as she repeated the process. 'Dear God, woman, what are you doing?'

'Torturing myself,' she said as she applied gel to a sponge and began working it into his shoulders.

'That makes two of us. If you have something important to tell me you'd better get on with it, while I can still think.'

'I've organised a cleaning party for the house. We'll be staying there from Saturday for the entire week.'

'Staying?' He half turned to look at her.

'Relax. It's just my family.' She worked the soap down his back, into the hollow above those gorgeous tight buttocks.

'No…' he began, then caught his breath as she used her hands to work the soap between his thighs.

'The Cornwall holiday fell through so I offered them a week in the country in return for a little light housework.'

'I can't ask your family to clean my house,' he said.

'You didn't—I did,' she said, getting down on her knees and working the foam behind his knees, over his totally gorgeous calves. 'Patsy's volunteered, too.'

'Patsy?'

'I saw her in the street. She said I should run that by you.'

'The whole damn street will know every detail within an hour of her coming home.'

'It's just an old house,' she reminded him. 'A lot of dull portraits, a couple of four-poster beds and a kitchen out of the Ark. I just need you to tell Ramsey and the security people that we'll be there,' she said. 'Now you can turn around.'

He turned and for a moment the breath stopped in her throat. He might not have been to bed in a week, but one part was still wide awake and ready for action.

Everything slowed down as she dropped the sponge and used her fingers between his toes, his ankles, the tender spot behind his knees, the smooth skin inside his thighs. Then she stood up and soaped his chest, his stomach.

At one point he reached for her but she tutted. 'No touching…'

His legs were trembling by the time she reached the parts that did not know when to lie down and quit.

'Sweet heaven,' he said, leaning back, clutching at a rack holding a pile of towels, his eyes closed as she took him in her palm, stroking him until, with a shuddering sigh, he spilled into her hand. And then she flipped off the water, put her arms around his neck and kissed him very gently. 'Now, go to bed.'

Darius, dazed, barely able to speak, reached up and pulled a towel down from the rack, wrapped it around her and pulled her warm, wet body against him. 'Stay with me,' he begged.

'Is that what a muse would do?' she asked, looking at him, her eyes dark, intense, searching. A smallest of frowns defeating her smile. 'Be there so that when you wake up you can draw her sated, replete, every desire satisfied?'

'I left a note,' he said. 'I left the picture…'

'Why?'

'You were sleeping. Taking it would have been as if I was stealing something intimate from you.'

'Oh.' She leaned her forehead against his chest so that

he shouldn't see her eyes. See what she had been thinking.
'If you want it, Darius, take it. It's yours.'

He took a step back, lifted her chin, reading her as easily as most people read headlines. 'You thought it was a
kiss off?' he asked. 'A Darius Hadley sketch in return for
some hot sex?'

'No! Maybe.' Her shoulders dropped. 'I don't know you,
Darius.'

'No, you don't,' he said, pulling another towel from the
rack, wrapped it around his waist. 'If I ever did anything
that skanky I would sign and date it so that it would be
worth something. A realisable asset.'

'Darius…'

He didn't wait for her mumbled apology. She hadn't
trusted him and that was a deal-breaker. He picked up the
receiver of the landline beside the bed, punched in a fast-
dial number.

'Ramsey? Darius Hadley.' He didn't bother with the
courtesies. 'My agent has organised a clean-up of the house.
Please inform the security people that they will be resident
on site from…' He looked across at Natasha, hovering in
the doorway of the wet room, a towel clutched to her breast.

'Today,' she said on a gasp. 'I'm going down there today
to turn on the water, clean up the—'

'From today,' he said, despite everything, unable to take
his eyes off her as Ramsey droned on about the inadvisabil-
ity of letting a group of strangers into the house. The damp
strands of hair clinging to pink cheeks, creamy shoulders
and it was all he could do to stop himself from going to
her. Begging forgiveness…

This was the madness. The same madness that had
seized his father. Wanting a woman beyond sense, beyond
reason.

'Your objections are noted but, to tell you the truth,
Ramsey,' he said, cutting him off, 'I don't actually care

what you think. The only reason I don't just sign the whole lot over to the Treasury is because someone has to protect the tenants and I know that won't be you.' He cut off Ramsey's protest. 'Is there anything else?' he asked, returning the receiver to the cradle, but leaving his hand on it, anchoring him to the spot.

Tash swallowed. His face was shuttered and the apology bubbling up in her throat died unspoken.

Shouting at him when he'd behaved like a jerk had been a momentary bump in the road, no more than a shake-up. Doubting his honour was, apparently, a damned great rock. She'd crossed some invisible line and the damage was terminal.

'There's just one more thing,' she said, clutching the towel to her breast. Being naked had, in an eye blink, gone from the most natural, most perfect thing in the world to the most awkward.

This definitely came under the 'never mix business with pleasure' rule but, despite the lack of encouragement to continue, there was still business to be done.

'Unlike Morgan and Black, I can't afford to put on a three-course lunch at the Hadley Arms, so I'm holding an open day on Saturday week,' she said. 'I'll be serving afternoon tea. On the lawn if the weather holds, in the ballroom if it doesn't.' There was still no response. Not even a sarcastic comment about cake. He just kept his hand on the phone as if waiting for her to go so that he could make another call. 'While I have no doubt that potential buyers and the property press would like to meet you, it's not essential.' Not one word. 'That's all.'

She gathered her clothes, made it downstairs on rubber legs, pulling them on over still damp skin as she headed for the door, banging it hard shut behind her. So that he'd know she'd gone. So that she couldn't go back.

Damn, damn, damn… How could she have got it so wrong? How could she have got herself so involved?

Involved was for the future, when she was established, with a man who was ready to settle down, raise a family. It wasn't for now and it certainly wasn't with a man who had heartbreak stamped all over him. She'd known from the first moment she'd set eyes on him that he wasn't a man made for happy ever after. This was supposed to be a fling. Hot, fast, furious and, like the bronze of an anonymous nude figure, something to rub your fingers over in passing when you were old and remember with a smile.

Okay. The bronze wasn't going to happen. Her career, on the other hand, still needed to be rescued. That deal was still on. It was back to strictly business.

Which was what she'd wanted in the first place. Until she didn't.

'Natasha?' She'd reached the corner of the street without being aware how she'd got there and practically bumped into Patsy as she came out of the corner shop carrying a bundle of files. 'Are you okay?'

'Oh, um, yes… Just in a hurry,' she said, suddenly aware of damp strands of hair clinging to her cheek and neck, that her top, pulled on over damp skin, was twisted, telegraphing what had just happened as loudly as if she'd posted his drawing on Facebook. 'There's so much to do. I, um, told Darius you had volunteered to join the clean-up party.'

'Let me guess. He said no.'

'No.' He hadn't. He'd muttered about gossip but he hadn't actually said no. Why would he? She'd been posting pictures of Hadley Chase all over the Net and there was nothing Patsy could tell the neighbours that they couldn't see for themselves. 'I'll be glad to have you if you're still up for it.'

'I'll be there, rubber gloves and dusters at the ready.'

'It won't all be work,' she assured her. 'Does your boy like fishing?'

She grinned. 'I guess we'll find out.'

Tash opened her bag and took out one of the new business cards she'd ordered off the Net—*Natasha Gordon, Property Consultant*—and offered it to Patsy. 'Email me if you have any special food requirements. And everyone is bringing their own bedding. Is that okay?'

'None and no problem. I'll come tomorrow afternoon straight after school if you like? Help you get the bedrooms ready.'

'You are such a star!'

'We'll be there at about six.'

'Great.' She was halfway around the corner when Patsy called, 'Natasha…' She half turned. 'Your skirt is caught up in your knickers.'

CHAPTER NINE

THE FIRST THING Tash did when she arrived at Hadley Chase was hunt down the stopcock in the scullery and turn the water on. It was, of course, stuck fast, so her next task was to brave the cobwebs and spiders in the toolshed to find a wrench so that she could shift it.

Someone had left all the taps open, which was obviously the right thing to do, but meant that once the tank had filled and the water was flowing she had to tour the house, turning them all off, mopping up leaks and making a note of where they were so that they could be fixed. A job for her dad, and she fired off a text to him, asking him to bring some plumber's mait.

She paused on the first floor landing, aware that something had changed but for a moment unable to think what it was. Then she realised that it was the window.

Despite working day and night to finish his sculpture, Darius had remembered his promise to get it fixed and for a moment she leaned her forehead against the cool surface of the glass. She had wanted him to trust her with the darkness that lay at his heart but she'd been so quick to leap to the conclusion that he was about as deep as an August puddle. And if he was, wasn't that what she'd expected? Gone into with her eyes wide open? Except he'd been angry, because… Well, because didn't matter.

Without trust there was nothing. And that was what she had. Nothing.

With a throat full of dust and desperate for a cup of tea, she plugged in the electric kettle. It blew a fuse. She mended it with the wire and screwdriver she'd brought with her. Next job, lighting the ancient solid fuel range cooker...

By the time she'd got it going, she was coated in smoke and black dust and more cobwebs from the fuel store, her knuckles were sore and she was seriously considering her mother's suggestion of an alternative career in the confectionery business.

Unfortunately, having spent the previous night emailing individual invitations to the open house and afternoon tea—spiced with the painting of the house and extracts from the history as attachments—to everyone she could think of, partners and children included since it was the weekend, any career change would have to be put on hold until she'd shifted two years' worth of dust.

The first job was the fridge. She washed it down, then switched it on. Another fuse blew, tripping all the electrics for the second time.

This time she went through them all, changing the wire in three that looked a bit dodgy. That done, she toured the house again, checking every light switch. The last thing she needed was to have them go pop when it was dark.

It was dark by the time she'd wiped down the last surface in the scullery. She picked up the bowl of water to tip down the sink and then screamed as she caught sight of a face in the window, slopping water down her filthy jeans and over her shoes in the process. Belatedly realising that it was her own face, smudged with coal dust, she laughed a little shakily. Then a second face appeared beside it.

This time the scream wouldn't come.

She opened her mouth, but her throat was stuffed with rocks and no sound emerged, even when the back door opened and a black-clad figure put his head around the door.

'Sorry, miss, I didn't mean to startle you.'

It was the security guard who'd tried to move them on.

'Mr Hadley called the office to tell us you'd be here and asked if I would look in on you and check that you were all right. He thought you'd be easier if it was someone you knew by sight.'

Since the rocks were taking their time to budge, she tipped the remaining water down the sink.

He shrugged awkwardly. 'I'm sorry about the other day.'

'No problem… Just doing your job… I'm fine,' she said, sounding unconvincing even to herself. 'Would you like a cup of tea?' she offered, peeling off her rubber gloves and squelching her way into the now gleaming kitchen.

'I can do better than that,' he said, placing a carrier on the table from which emerged the mouth-watering scent of hot fried food and the sharpness of vinegar.

Until that moment she hadn't thought of food but, suddenly assailed by sharp pangs of hunger, she said, 'Please tell me that's fish and chips.'

He grinned. 'Mr Hadley thought you might be glad of something hot to eat.'

Darius… Her heart, just about back to normal, missed a beat. She'd said she didn't know him, but it seemed that he knew her.

'There appear to be two lots,' she said, peering into the carrier.

'Well, I haven't had my supper yet. I was going to have it in the van, but why don't I put the kettle on while you dry off?'

It was barely light when Darius woke, fully aroused—he'd been dreaming about Natasha. One moment she'd been a vision in something floaty, looking and smelling like a summer garden, the next she'd been pressed up against him, naked, soapy wet, her fingers kneading his scalp, her breasts against his back. And when he'd turned round and she'd taken him in her hand...

He closed his eyes, wanting that moment back. Wanting her to be there with him. He'd asked her to stay, but then...

Then he'd done what he always did with any woman who got too close, who he wanted too much; he'd used the first excuse that offered itself to make it impossible for her to stay.

She was so easy to read. Every thought, every idea was right there in her lovely face and she knew it. The fact that she'd buried her face in his chest was enough to warn him that she was hiding something and damn it, of course he was mad that she could think such a thing of him. But why wouldn't she?

She'd just been betrayed in the worst possible way. Her confidence had to be shaky. And he'd made all kinds of excuses not to wake her because she could read him, too. Would have seen what he could not hide. That it had been a panic run.

What he'd felt, what he'd drawn, had terrified him. He'd had to leave her a note so that she knew about the Land Rover and keys, but it had been bare of emotion. He'd left mixed messages and she'd interpreted them just as he'd hoped she would. Until he'd walked around that truck and his heart had practically leapt out of his chest with joy.

He knew what he felt was senseless. And he'd acted senselessly.

He took a cup of coffee out into the tiny yard he shared with a couple of randy pigeons and a pot of dead daffodils, watching the sun turn the sky from a pale grey to blue, stirring only when there was a long peal on the doorbell.

It was Patsy with a large cardboard envelope. It was addressed to him c/o Patsy and when he turned it over, saw it was from Natasha, he didn't have to open it to know what it was.

'I don't know you...'

Of course she didn't. He'd never let anyone close enough to know him. He didn't know himself.

'Why did she send it to you?' he asked. 'How did she know your address?'

'I don't keep it a secret,' she said, looking pointedly at his door. The cottage, like the studio, bore no number. 'She's a nice woman, Darius.'

'No...' There were a dozen words rushing into his head to describe Natasha, but 'nice' wasn't one of them. Vivid, fun, kind, thoughtful, vulnerable, hot, glorious, spicy sweet... He realised that Patsy was looking at him a little oddly. 'Sorry, yes, of course you're right.'

'I'm going to Hadley Chase as soon as school is out this afternoon. When will you be coming down?'

'I have to go to the foundry today,' he said. 'Take the horse apart so that they can start making the moulds.' Dozens of intricate parts, every one of which had to be checked for imperfections through each stage of the process.

'And tomorrow?' she asked.

'It's going to take weeks,' he said, but she knew that. That wasn't what she was asking.

She didn't press it. 'Any message?'

He shook his head. 'No, wait.' He took a card out of his wallet and handed it to her. 'Pay for the food. And whatever's needed for the open house party. Tell them to help themselves to whatever wine is left in the cellar.'

'Is that it?'

'Michael will find it very different,' he said, reluctant to let her go, disapproval in every line. She knew how he was. That he never got involved.

'That's the point of a holiday,' she said and—for the first time since he'd known her—she refused the opportunity to talk at length about her son, about anything and left him standing on his doorstep.

He closed the door, opened the envelope, took out the drawing and traced every line of Natasha's spicy sweet sleeping body with his finger.

Sated, replete, every desire satisfied...

'Not just you, Sugarlips,' he murmured. 'Not just you.'

Natasha opened her eyes and lay quite still, not sure for a moment where she was. Then, as everything came into focus and she saw the distant hills through a tall window, she remembered. She was at Hadley Chase, lying in the bed that Darius Hadley had slept in as a boy.

She'd crawled into it some time after midnight, every limb aching, too exhausted to bother with the curtains— nothing but a passing owl would see her—and curled into his pillow, wishing he was there with her.

No chance.

For a while she'd been warmed by the fact that he'd asked the security people to check on her, bring her something hot to eat—he must have known that the old range cooker wouldn't deliver on day one—and she had sent a text, thanking him. Nothing fancy.

Thanks for supper. Most welcome. T

No more, no less than any well brought-up woman would do.

There was no response. Of course not. You didn't expect a reply to a bread-and-butter thank-you note. The food, she reminded herself, had been no more than a courtesy. She might have mortally offended his sense of honour, but she had organised a freebie clean-up of his house: *noblesse oblige* and all that.

She reached for her phone, kidding herself she was

checking the time—hoping that he might have unbent suf-
ficiently to ask if she was okay in the empty silence of the
night.

Nothing. No texts. No missed calls.

She sighed, rolled out of bed, winced a little as she stood
up. Her knees creaked and her shoulder hurt from all the
stretching and bending and scrubbing, but at least there
was hot water for a shower.

She stoked up the oven, took a cup of tea out into the
garden and sat on a bench beneath a climbing rose massed
with creamy buds. A small muntjac doe with a tiny fawn
wandered across the lawn within feet of her. She took a photograph with her phone and Tweeted it—there was nothing like cute animals to get a response—not forgetting to
add the website URL.

Her mother and sisters-in-law would arrive with a ton of
food, she knew, but ten adults and eight children were going
to take a lot of feeding so she headed to the village to make
the day of the butcher and the couple who ran the village
store and farm shop. Orders placed, she treated herself to
coffee and a muffin at the pub while she took advantage of
their free Wi-Fi to check her Facebook and Twitter pages.

There were a couple of messages on Facebook asking
her to get in touch, one from a publisher, the other from the
features editor of a magazine, both asking her to ring them.

They were both interested in Emma Hadley's history
of Hadley Chase so she invited them to the open house on
Saturday. Maybe she should invite Freddie, the art dealer,
too. If she could sell the book, the paintings and the house
in one day she would become a legend.

Meanwhile, acceptances to the open house were coming in; even the regional television news magazine were
hoping to send a team. No response yet from the *Country
Chronicle* despite personal notes to both the editor and the

advertising manager who, in her opinion, owed Darius a two-page feature at the very least.

She checked a missed call from her mother, a response to the text to her Dad. She'd left a voicemail expressing disbelief that her daughter had spent the night alone in a house that was miles from anywhere. If she'd known, if she'd *told* her, she stressed, she would have come on ahead of her father.

Normally the suggestion that she couldn't cope would have infuriated her. Instead, she found herself in total agreement. Last night, she would have totally welcomed her mother's company. She was smiling at that thought when she realised that someone was standing on the far side of the table.

Expecting it to be the girl wanting to clear her coffee, she said, 'I'm done.' Then, when she didn't begin to clear she looked up and her heart stopped.

'Darius...' Her vocal cords seemed to be in some disarray, too. 'I...um... How did you get here?'

'I took a train to Swindon,' he said, 'and then caught the bus. Piece of cake.'

He should have smiled then, but he didn't.

'You've still got Gary's car,' she said as her brain, buffering the emotion dump, the rush of sensations, images of him racing through her memory like a speeded-up film, finally caught up.

'It needed servicing.'

'Don't tell me,' she said, 'you're not just Darius Hadley, sculptor. You moonlight as Mike, the man who repairs cars while you wait.'

Smile now. Smile, pull out a chair, sit down, tell me why you're here. Please...

'I spotted the Land Rover as I drove through the village.' No smile. Still standing.

'I've been organising supplies for the week and stopped

to use the Wi-Fi.' She gestured vaguely at the open laptop. 'If you're stopping, will you sit down? I'm getting a crick in my neck.'

He pulled out the chair opposite and one of his knees brushed against hers as he sat down but he moved it before she could catch her breath and shift hers.

'Would you like some coffee?' she asked.

He shook his head.

Could this be any more awkward?

'I've…um…got a publisher interested in your grand-mother's history,' she said, her legs trembling with the strain as she tucked her feet back as far as they would go so that she didn't accidentally touch him.

'Then my troubles are over.'

Sarcasm she could do without. This she could do without.

'Why are you here, Darius?'

'Why did you send the drawing back?'

Oh, shoot. That was so complicated, so mixed up, such an emotional reaction…

'Why didn't you just tear it up?' he insisted, looking straight into her eyes. 'Throw it in the trash with the tea-bags and potato peelings.'

She blew out her cheeks, tucked a strand of hair behind her ear. 'It was a beautiful drawing, Darius. There was no way I could have destroyed it.'

The truth, plain and simple.

'You could have taken it to your friendly art dealer,' he said.

'Unsigned?'

'With a letter from you as provenance, he would have snatched your hand off.'

'No!' Her protest was instinctive. She could never share such an intimate moment with Freddie, or any other art dealer.

'You could have simply kept it,' he persisted.

'Something to shock the grandchildren?'

It was the second time she'd offered him a chance to smile at the memory of an earlier, happier moment. For the second time he did not take it, but simply waited, demanding total honesty, the exposure of feelings she'd been unwilling to even think because once you'd thought them...

'You left me something of yourself, Darius. A memory to treasure.' Explaining this was like tearing away layers of flesh. Total exposure of the inner depths he talked about. But infinitely safer than thoughts that even now were rushing in. 'I lost the right to anything so precious when I destroyed that with my lack of trust.'

'Trust is a two-way thing, Natasha.'

'You took me on trust, no questions asked.'

'That was business. This...'

She'd asked herself what it had taken to build that impenetrable façade. What it would take to shatter it. Suddenly, in that hesitation, she had a glimpse into the darkness. Trust. It was all about trust.

'This?'

He shook his head. 'You shared your past with me, Natasha, offered me the chance to open up to you, but I didn't have your courage.'

'No...' She instinctively reached out a hand to him, grasped his fingers. 'It's hard. It wasn't the moment. I understood.'

'And I understand about the drawing. If it hadn't mattered, you'd have either kept it as a souvenir of a hot night, or you'd have been checking out the value with Freddie Glover.'

'If it hadn't mattered,' she replied, 'you wouldn't have been so angry.'

And for a moment they both just sat there, looking at each other, aware that they had just crossed some line.

Then he turned his hand beneath hers so that their fingers were interlocked.

'I've been walking away from people since I was seventeen years old,' he said. 'I keep trying to walk away from you.'

'Why?'

'Is there anything in the Land Rover that will spoil if it's left for an hour or two?' he asked, ignoring the question. She shook her head. He stood up, closed up her laptop and took it across to the bar. 'Will you look after this, Peter?'

He nodded. 'It's been a while, Darius.'

'Too long,' he said, heading for the door. 'We'll catch up later.'

'Darius…' she protested. 'My entire life depends on my laptop!'

'It'll be safer there than left in the car. I'll come back for them both later.'

'Yes, but…'

'I walked away from Hadley Chase. I have to walk back.' He'd reached the doorway, looked back, held out his hand to her. 'Will you walk with me?'

'Why me, Darius?' she asked, taking it.

'I don't know,' he said, and finally there was the hint of a smile. 'Only that no one else will do.'

He said nothing more until they were through the open gates of Hadley Chase and walking down the path that led to the river.

'The Clarendon family used to live over there,' he said, pausing at a gap between the trees and looking across the river to where a four-square Georgian house nestled beneath a rise in the Downs. 'The families were very close. My father and Christabel Clarendon were practically betrothed in their prams.'

His father… 'The house is the headquarters of an IT firm now,' she said. 'Steve told me.'

'Steve?'

'The security guy. They had a false alarm there last night.' She turned to look up at him. 'Betrothed?'

'They were both only children,' he said, moving on. 'There was land and money on both sides and it was the perfect match.'

'It takes a bit more than that.'

'Does it? Arranged marriages are the norm in other cultures and they'd known one another since they were children. There would be no surprises.'

'There are always surprises.'

'Yes…' They were climbing now through the woods and he stopped before an ancient beech tree that had once been coppiced and had four thick trunks twisting from its base. He looked up. 'It's still here. The tree house.'

He put a foot on a trunk that had been cut to form steps and, catching a low branch, pulled himself up to take a look, then disappeared inside.

'Is it safe?' she asked, following him. 'Wow… This is some tree house.'

'Gary built it for me,' he said.

'Gary?' The floor was solid planks of timber, the roof a thick thatch where swallows had once nested, the sides made from canvas that rolled up. There was a rug and a pile of cushions, faded, torn, chewed or pecked. 'Why?'

'His dad worked on the estate. Gamekeeper, gardener, whatever needed to be done. When Gary left school, he became his dad's assistant and did odd jobs around the estate. One of those odd jobs was to keep me amused during the school holidays. One summer he amused me by building this.'

'He did a great job.'

'It was more than a job. He was like an older brother,' he said. 'The kind that teaches you all the good stuff. The stuff that adults tell you is bad for you.'

'Drinking, lads' mags, smoking the occasional spliff? I've got brothers,' she reminded him when his eyebrows rose. 'You can't know how much I wished I was a boy.'

'Can I say, just for the record, that I'm glad you're not?'

'Oh, me too,' she assured him. 'Men wear such boring shoes.'

He looked down at the purple ballet pumps she was wearing. 'Pretty.'

For a moment she had a vision of him bending down, taking one off, kissing her instep... She cleared her throat. 'What did you do up here?'

'When I was younger I used it the way any kid would. Hideout, den, a place to keep secret stash. We used to sit up here watching badgers at dusk.'

'Brilliant.'

'It was... Of course, Gary never put that much effort into anything without an ulterior motive. When I was away at school, he brought girls here.' He shrugged. 'I did too, when I was older.'

'The young master seducing the village maidens?' she teased.

'Rather the opposite,' he said and his sudden grin sent a lump to her throat for a magical youth that had been somehow blighted. 'I'll check it out, clean it up for your nephews and nieces.'

'Does that mean you're staying?'

'I've put off the foundry until Monday but they can't start without me. Is there room?' he said, sliding his arms around her waist, drawing her close, and the down on her cheeks stood up as if she were a magnet and he was the North Pole.

'No problem. I'll share. Your room is pretty much as you left it, give or take a few things. I borrowed some of the chocolate-box pictures for the blog. I've had a lot of interest,' she rushed on, to cover just how important his answer was. 'There's a greeting card manufacturer...'

'That's the take,' he said, ignoring the throwaway distraction. 'What's the give?'

'Me,' she said. 'If there's still a vacancy for a muse?'

'So when you said share...?'

'I could bunk in with Patsy, but I barely know her, while we're—'

He groaned, pulling her into his arms, kissing her with a hot, sweet, haunting tenderness that could rip the heart out of you. It was the perfect kiss you saw in the movies, the kiss a girl dreamed about before life gave you a reality check, the kiss you'd remember when every other memory had slipped away into the dark. When he finally drew back, rested his forehead against the top of her head, he was trembling.

'Darius...' She cradled his face in her hands, wanting to reassure him, to tell him... 'You kept the beard,' she said shakily.

She felt him smile against her palms. 'You said you liked it.'

'As I was saying, we're compatible in practically every way.'

'I doubt your parents would be impressed with our, um, compatibility,' he said, climbing down the tree, lifting her after him. 'And then there are those three over-protective brothers of yours. I'm seriously outnumbered.'

'That's ridiculous, Darius. It's your house.'

'No. I'll get a room at the pub.' He took her hand and began to walk up the path towards the house. 'I thought we might go back to the beginning, slow things down a little. Maybe date?'

'Date?'

'An old-fashioned concept, involving the back seat of the movies, Sunday lunch in a country pub, dancing.'

'You dance?'

'I can learn.'

'Well, perfect, but what about the muse thing?'

'Getting naked? Inspirational sex?' He grinned. 'We can do that too.' They had reached the edge of the lawn and they both turned to look at the house. 'We appear to have company,' he said as they spotted the small red car at the same moment that the woman leaning against it spotted them.

'Brace up, Darius. It's my mother.'

CHAPTER TEN

'MUM!' TASH GAVE her a hug. 'How lovely! Can I introduce Darius Hadley, the owner of Hadley Chase?'

'Mr Hadley.' Her mother's eyebrows remained exactly where they were. It just felt as if they'd done an imitation of Tower Bridge.

'Darius,' he said, offering his hand with a smile Tash recognised from the pages of the *Country Chronicle*. Protective camouflage that he wore in public, but never with her. 'I can't tell you how grateful I am to you for pitching in and helping like this.'

'I'm helping my daughter,' she said. 'I thought you were on your own, Tash, or I wouldn't have been so concerned.'

'I was and, believe me, if you'd had any idea you would have been a lot more concerned. Three electrical blowouts, a gazillion spiders and the fright of my life when the security guard peered in through the window.'

'Well, really! How thoughtless.'

'No…thoughtful. Darius was concerned about me, too, so he called their office and asked if Steve could bring me some fish and chips. He was perfectly sweet. He made up the Aga, made sure I knew how to set the alarm and checked all the outbuildings before he left.'

'I'm really glad you're here, Mrs Gordon,' Darius said before she could comment. 'I didn't think I'd be able to get away, but I've put back the project I'm working on until Monday. I met Natasha in the village just now when I stopped to book a room at the pub.'

'He's just shown me the most amazing tree house, Mum,' she said, taking out the keys and unlocking the front door and, just like that, they were through it and in the hall; no drama about the big moment when he stepped back into the house. 'The kids are going to love it. I'll make some coffee. Why don't you show my mother the portrait of Emma Hadley, Darius?' she suggested, pushing him in a little deeper. He glanced at her, the only sign of tension a touch of white around his mouth. 'She's going to give a talk to the Women's Institute on the history of this place.'

'Of course. It's in the library, Mrs Gordon,' he said.

'Laura,' she said. 'I don't understand. Why are you staying in the village?'

'Well, obviously I'll be here, doing as much as I can, but this is your holiday. You won't want a stranger—'

'Nonsense! Of course you must stay here.'

Tash grinned. *Bazinga…*

'Mum, Mum, we've found a boathouse! There's a single scull!'

Patsy rolled her eyes. 'I told you not to go near the river without an adult, Michael.'

'Tom and Harry and James are down there, river dipping with the little kids.'

'Are you interested in rowing, Michael?' Darius, who was cutting the lawn, had stopped for a drink of the fresh lemonade Patsy had brought out.

'He's been desperate to try it ever since the Games,' she said.

'Well, let's go and take a look at it. I'll need a hand to get it down. Any volunteers?' He glanced around at the women stretched out on the grass, soaking up the sun, studiously avoiding looking at Natasha, who took the view that the one-hour rule didn't apply to her and was busy washing down the external doors and windowsills.

'Take Tash,' Patsy suggested. 'Please. She's making us feel guilty.'

'Natasha?' he prompted. 'Do you want to give these women a break?'

'They're on holiday, I'm not.' But she peeled off her rubber gloves and joined him.

'Did you sleep well?' he asked as they followed Michael down to the river.

'Not especially,' she admitted. 'You'd think in a house of this size we might manage a few minutes on our own. If the kids had been ordered to chaperone us, they couldn't have done a better job of it.'

'Your mother knew what she was doing when she insisted I stay,' he said. 'If it's any consolation, I'm not getting much sleep, either.'

'Memories?' she asked.

'More the fact that my childhood bed no longer smells of dog, but of you. Which is very disturbing, especially when I've spent the last twenty-four hours under the close-eyed scrutiny of your three very large brothers who, let me tell you, are nowhere as easy to charm as your mother.'

'Maybe you should stop being so charming to their wives,' she suggested, a little tetchily, he thought.

'You want me to be charming to you?'

'No! That is so not what I want and you know it.'

He knew but they'd reached the boathouse and Michael was dancing with impatience, waiting for the slowcoach adults to catch up.

'Anticipation only increases the gratification,' he said.

'That had better be a promise.'

'Cross my heart,' he said, drawing a cross over his chest, just as she had, and she groaned.

'Come on!'

'Okay, let's see.'

The buckles on the straps were rusted but they finally managed to free them and lower the scull into the water and then watch as it filled with water.

'I'm sorry, Mike; the hull is cracked.'

'Can it be fixed?' he asked once they hauled it out of the water and Darius had located the damage.

'Maybe, but it's a fibreglass hull and will have to go to a special workshop.' Seeing his disappointment, he said, 'You know, if you're really keen on trying this, Michael, I'll find you a club in London where you can get some proper training.'

The boy's mouth dropped open. 'Wicked!'

'You'd better go and ask your mother. Tell her that it's my contribution to the medal tally in 2020,' he called after him.

Natasha was grinning. 'He's a great kid.'

'Patsy worries about him. I think that's why she volunteered for your work party. She can't watch him twenty-four-seven and he's getting to the age for trouble.'

'Sport is a good alternative.' She looked at the scull. 'Was this yours?'

'It belonged to my father. He was a rowing blue. When I was a kid like Michael, I used to sit in that seat, put my feet and hands where his had been and try to feel him.'

'You never knew him?' she asked.

He shook his head. 'He was a lecturer at the School of Oriental and African Studies. He lived there during the week and came home to the estate cottage where he and Christabel had set up home for the weekends and during the holiday.'

'That doesn't sound like a great way to start a marriage.'

'It was her choice, apparently. She didn't like London.'

'What happened?'

'Not a what—a who. An Iranian student of such shimmering beauty that one look was all it took for my father to lose his head, his reason, his sanity.'

'Your mother.' And, when he glanced at her, 'The name is the giveaway.'

He nodded. 'My father abandoned Christabel and his unborn child without a backward glance and went to live in France with Soraya.'

Unable to bear the musty boathouse, the memory of that boy trying to reach out to a father he'd never known, he walked out into the clean air, kicked off his shoes and sat on the crumbling dock. These days his feet trailed in the water, soaked into the bottom of his jeans.

Natasha picked her way carefully over the boards and sat down beside him, her toes trailing in the water, waiting for him to continue or not as he wished.

'My grandfather cut him off without a penny, hoping it would bring him to his senses,' he said. 'But he was senseless.'

'And Christabel? What did she do?'

'She took it badly, lost the baby she was carrying. A boy who would have been the heir to all this.'

'Poor woman…'

'Her parents sold the house across the river and moved away. Gary told me that she'd killed herself.'

'No!'

'My grandfather denied it but I was never sure so I did a search a few years back.' He plucked a piece of rotten wood from the plank beside him, shredded it, dropping the pieces in the water. 'She lives in Spain with her husband, three children.'

'Did you get in touch with her?'

'I wanted to. I wanted to talk to someone who'd known my father so I went to the house, hoping to see her. They were just going out…' He shook his head. 'Rumour always has a grain of truth. She might have tried something desperate and she didn't need me descending like a black crow in the midst of her lovely family, raking up the past.'

Tash felt tears sting the back of her eyes and the lump in her throat was so big that she couldn't say anything. Instead, she squeezed his hand.

He glanced at her. 'Is that approval? I got something right?'

'Absolutely.' She slid her arm around his waist and he put his arm around her shoulders so that her head was resting against his shoulder. 'What happened to your parents?' Something bad must have happened or he wouldn't have been living with his grandparents.

'When I was a few months old, Soraya's mother became desperately ill and she had to go home. She left me with my father, which seems a little odd, but they weren't married and maybe she was afraid to tell her family that she was living with a married man. That they had a child.'

'I think I'd find that pretty difficult, to be honest.'

'It seems they already knew. Two days after she left, my father received a message from her father. He wanted to bring his family to Europe and, to get exit visas, they needed money to bribe officials. A lot of money. The bottom line was that if he wanted to see Soraya again he would have to pay.'

'But…that's appalling!'

'My father, beside himself, went to my grandfather, begged him for help and the old bastard gave it to him, but at a price.'

'You…' She'd known there was something, but could never have guessed anything so desperate. So cruel.

'He'd lost his heir. His son was unfit in his eyes. I wasn't the golden child of the perfect marriage, but I was all he had left.'

'You were the price he had to pay to rescue your mother.'

'Ramsey drew up a legally binding document surrendering all parental rights to them. I was to live with my grandparents, they would have full control of my education and upbringing and I would be my grandfather's heir on the condition that my parents understood that they would be dead to me. And my father signed it.'

'Of course he signed. How could he do anything else? He loved your mother, Darius; he couldn't abandon her.'

'No. I was safe and she needed him.'

A kingfisher flashed from a post into the water. A duck rounded up her fluffy brood. Somewhere along the river-bank a child shrieked with excitement. All bright, wonderful things, but what had been a charmed day now had a dark edge to it.

'What happened?' she asked.

'My grandfather handed over the cash, my father left for the airport and that's the last anyone ever heard of him or my mother. Not that anyone was looking.'

'I'm so sorry.'

'When he died, I insisted that Ramsey carry out a proper search for them before the house was put on the market. If either of them were alive this belonged to them.'

'Was there nothing in the house you could sell?'

'Unfortunately, the Hadleys weren't great art collectors. No one had the foresight to commission Gainsborough to paint the family portraits, buy Impressionists when they were cheap, snap up a Picasso or two.'

'Ancestors can be so short-sighted. What about land? Or the cottages?'

'The land is green belt and can't be built on. The cottages are occupied by former members of staff. I'll use what's left from the sale to rehouse them.'

'And the London flat?'

'When he was diagnosed with Alzheimer's, Ramsey insisted my grandfather sign a power of enduring attorney in my name. I sold the flat to finance his nursing care. There's some money left, but not enough to pay the inheritance tax.'

'Your grandfather might have raised you, Darius Hadley, but you are nothing like him.'

'At seventeen I was halfway there. Arrogant, spoilt, thought I owned the world. If I'd stayed here, I would have been exactly like him.'

She wanted to tell him he was wrong. She just tightened her hold around his waist and for a moment he buried his face in her hair. After a while, he said, 'My grandmother came to my first exhibition. She was dying by then, but she defied him that once. I went to her funeral but when my grandfather saw me he thought I was my father and began ranting at me...'

'Did Ramsey discover any more about what happened to your parents?' she said, desperate to distract him from the horror of that image.

'Only rumours. That the family had been caught trying to leave the country and they were all either rotting in jail or dead. That my father had made the whole story up just to get his hands on the money and he and Soraya were living somewhere in the sun. That my father was the victim of a honeypot trap and once he'd handed over the money he was disposed of. Take your pick.'

'No. Not the last one.'

And for the first time the smallest hint of a smile softened his face. 'You know that for a fact, do you?'

'One hundred per cent,' she said. 'Maybe, for a passion so intense that nothing else mattered they might have surrendered their son. Considered it their penance. But if it had been a con, Soraya would have got rid of you the second she realised she was pregnant.'

Totally focused on him, on his pain, she saw the gone-in-a-moment swirl of emotion deep in his eyes; scudding clouds of joy, sorrow, dark and light, every shade of grey.

'You didn't know any of this? Growing up?' He shook his head. 'Gary. Gary told you.' Who else? 'Was it one too many beers on one of your owl-or badger-watching adventures?'

'It wasn't beer that loosened his tongue. It was a motorbike. He had an old bike that he'd rebuilt from scrap and he taught me to ride when I was barely tall enough to reach the pedals. When I got a brand-new bike for my seventeenth birthday he was the first person I wanted to share it with.'

'Oh...' She could see what was coming.

'Young, brash, spoilt, it never occurred to me how he would feel. Obviously, I'd always had more than him, but this was grown-up stuff, stuff he wanted and could never afford on the pittance my grandfather paid him. Stuff I didn't have to work for, but would come to me just because my name was Hadley. It was like a chasm had opened up between us and he lashed out with the only weapon he had to put himself back on top. It just came out. How my father had sold me so that he could be with his whore.'

'Chinese whispers,' she said, perfectly able to imagine how gossip whispered in the village had been distorted, twisted with every retelling. Garbled, warped...

'He was already back-pedalling, trying to take it back before I'd fired up the bike to go and confront my grandfather, but nothing could unsay those words. I demanded to know the truth and the old man didn't spare me. He said I was old enough to know the truth and he laid it out in black and white. My father had betrayed his wife, abandoned his unborn child for a—'

'Darius...'

She'd cut in, not wanting him to repeat the word, but he raised his hand to touch her cheek, looked down at her. 'Let me finish. Get it out in the light.' He made a gesture that took in the sagging boathouse, the house out of sight behind the trees. 'This is all he really cared about. Preserv-

ing the house, preserving the name. Nothing that was real.'
He took his wallet from his back pocket, opened it, handed
her a photograph. 'This is what my father cared about.'

'She's beautiful, Darius.' The snapshot was of a young
woman laughing at something the photographer had said,
her eyes filled with so much love that it took her breath
away. To be looked at like that... 'Where did you get this?'

'It arrived in an envelope after my grandmother came
to the exhibition. No note.'

'A smile like that against four hundred years of history. No contest.' She looked up at Darius, at the same
dark eyes... 'She would have come for you. Crawled over
broken glass. No piece of paper would have stopped her.'

'Yes. I've always known, deep down, that they're dead
but I hoped...'

'Where did you go? How did you live?' she asked.
'When you left?'

'Not in a cardboard box under Waterloo Bridge,' he said,
apparently reading her mind. 'I went to Bristol, sold the
bike, rented a room, signed on at a sixth form college and
got a job stacking supermarket shelves.'

'The *bike*?' she said. 'You told me you walked out!'

'Metaphorically,' he said, but the darkness had been replaced with the beginnings of a smile. 'I wanted...I needed
you to walk with me.'

'All you had to do was ask.' For a moment they just
looked at one another until it was too intense, too full of
the unspoken words in her head and she scrambled for another thought. 'What happened to Gary?' she asked, her
voice catching in her throat.

'You always go straight to the heart of what's important, Natasha. I'm banging on about ancient history and
you bring me crashing back to earth with what's real. The
human element.'

'I wasn't dismissing what happened to you. But you said

it, Darius. You had everything going for you while he had nothing and I can't imagine your grandfather was a man to overlook such an indiscretion.'

'You're right, of course. I didn't betray Gary but it couldn't have been anyone else. Mary told me that my grandfather gave him a choice—he left the estate and never returned, or his father and grandmother would lose their jobs and the cottages that went with them.'

'Hurting, angry, lashing out... He made them all pay.'

'If I'd stayed I could have stopped that.'

'How? By bargaining with him? What would you have surrendered to save him?' He had no answer to that. 'He would have had you at his mercy, Darius. You were both better off away from here.'

'Right again. My mistake was not stopping to pick up Gary on the way out. I'll always regret that.'

'I don't imagine you were thinking very clearly,' she said, untangling herself from his arms. 'Come on,' she said, standing up, picking up her shoes. 'There's grass to cut, doors to be washed...'

Darius caught her hand. 'Thank you.'

There was nothing she could think of to say, so she stood on her toes and kissed him. It was supposed to be brief, sweet, over in a moment, but neither of them wanted it to stop. Even when the kiss was over they didn't want to let go.

'If we don't go back soon, they'll wonder where we are.'

'You wanted to take a good look at the boathouse, check if it will have to be pulled down or whether it can be re-stored,' he offered.

'Right,' she said, leaning her forehead against his chest before forcing herself to step away, get back to washing down paintwork. When she turned around her brother James was leaning on the wall of the boathouse, arms folded over the fishing rod he was holding. He'd clearly been there for some time.

CHAPTER ELEVEN

DARIUS WAS THE first to recover. 'Did you manage to catch supper?' he asked.

'With half a dozen children screaming and splashing about? They've scared away every fish within five miles so we thought we'd leave the women to sort out lunch while we walk down to the village and test the local ale. It's a Sunday holiday tradition. There'll be a pint waiting when you've finished checking out the structural integrity of the boathouse.'

He didn't wait for an answer.

'Did that sound like a friendly invitation,' Darius asked, 'or am I going to be pinned to the dartboard?'

'The pre-Sunday lunch trip to the pub is a mysterious male tradition,' she replied, 'from which mothers, wives and sisters are excluded. All I can tell you with any certainty is that you're the first man I've kissed who's ever been invited by my brothers to join them.'

'So that's good?'

'Probably, but if they do pin you to the dartboard by your ears I'll give them all particularly noxious jobs tomorrow.'

'I'll want pictures,' he said.

'I'll post them on Facebook,' she promised. 'When are you leaving?'

'After lunch. I've got to do what I should have done on Friday before the foundry starts up on Monday morning.

I can't promise to be here on Saturday. Once we start, we don't stop until it's done.'

'I didn't expect you to come this weekend. It's been...'

'Fun, Natasha. It's been fun.'

'Even getting beaten by my mother at Scrabble?' He said nothing. 'You let her win? Go!' she said, laughing, pushing him away. 'Before your beer gets warm.'

Before she dragged him under the nearest bush.

Darius, pausing for a break, checked his phone. There was a text from Natasha.

Needs full structural survey. Xxx

She'd attached a photograph of the boathouse.

Grinning, he took a selfie and sent it back with a text.

Needs total scrub down. Xxx

Natasha had kept in touch, sending pictures of the house emerging from its cocoon, but it was her suggestive little texts that made him smile. He'd replied with pictures of bones emerging from moulds. No comment needed.

Tash sighed with pleasure. Hadley Chase was gleaming, as perfect as she could have hoped, brought back to life, not just by sunlight and polish, but the laughter of children, the smell of baking, the armfuls of flowers from the long neglected cutting garden supplemented by cow parsley, willow herb gathered by her sisters-in-law to create huge free-form flower arrangements.

Tables had been laid in the conservatory for tea, the hired water boiler and teapots lined up and ready, the doors thrown open to the lawn, where the children were playing croquet with a set Harry had found in one of the outbuildings as the first cars began to arrive.

'It looks magical, Tash. If Darius were here he wouldn't be able to let this go,' Patsy said.

'Maybe that's why he's staying away.'

'Or not. Isn't that his Land Rover?' Patsy had offered to drive her home so that he could take the Land Rover back to London. 'Go and say hello,' she said as he drove straight round to the back of the house.

'Too late,' she said as the editor of the *Country Chronicle* advanced towards her, hand outstretched.

'Tash! I'm so glad to see you looking so well.'

'As you can see, Kevin, rumours of my breakdown were not just exaggerated but completely untrue.' She took his hand. 'Thank you for coming today. It means a great deal to me.'

'You have Peter Black to thank for that. He is so angry with you that he threatened to withdraw all Morgan and Black advertising if I covered the Hadley Chase open day.'

'A bit of a hollow threat, I'd have thought. There is nowhere else for this kind of property.'

'Hollow or not, I can't allow advertisers to dictate what we print.' He looked around. 'I have to congratulate you, my dear; your campaign has caused quite a stir. The children are a nice touch, by the way. Can we photograph them with the house in the background for our feature?'

'Feature?'

He smiled. 'Two pages? Maybe more if Darius Hadley will talk to me. I don't like being threatened.'

Darius stood back, watching Natasha greet visitors, delegate various members of her family to show them around the house, confident, professional, totally focused on the task she'd set herself. She'd told him she was the best and she was right. For a while she'd been entirely his but after this her world would reclaim her.

It was what he'd wanted, he reminded himself. It was the way he always wanted things. A hot flirtation and then move on. No emotional engagement.

Too late. It had been too late the moment he'd set eyes

on her, too late the minute he'd allowed her to stay. Kissed her. He'd let down his guard, done what he'd sworn he'd never do. He'd fallen hopelessly, ridiculously in love and where once he would have thought that made him a fool, he now knew that it made him a better man.

The thought made him smile and he was just going to her, to tell her that, when Morgan appeared on the doorstep. He instinctively took a step forward to protect her, but she had it covered, her voice clear, calm, composed.

'Miles? This is unexpected.'

'I'm here to apologise, Tash. I've been made a fool of.'

'Really?' She didn't step back to let him inside.

'That idiot Toby has gone.'

'Gone?' That rattled the cool.

'He's signed a contract to play professional rugby in Italy. It seems that's where he was last month. Not on a tour, but having trials, medicals, negotiating a deal. When his parents found out they were furious so they cooked up this scheme to cause a crisis, get rid of you and force him to forget the sports nonsense and put the company, his family first. He arrived at the reception not knowing what the hell was going on, but his mother cried and he was cornered.'

'Why on earth couldn't they just let him be happy?'

'Families, inheritance...' He shrugged. 'You know how it is.'

'Yes...' she said. 'Yes, I know.' She cleared her throat. 'Was Janine involved?'

'She and Peter were always...close. Let's just say that she's currently seeking alternative career opportunities.'

'And what about Morgan and Black?' she asked.

'There is no Black. That is the second reason I'm here. I'm looking for a new partner, Tash. I would like it to be you.'

Darius didn't wait for her answer. He'd just heard the

sound of hell freezing over and he'd felt the chill to his bones.

He hoped to escape unnoticed but Laura was in the kitchen, loading up a trolley with sandwiches, cakes, scones.

'Darius! How lovely to see you. Does Tash know you're here?'

He shook his head. 'She's busy.'

'Is it going well out there?'

'There seem to be a lot of people. Can I give you a hand?'

'I've got it covered. Why don't you take a last look around while the house is looking at its best? The way it must have been when you lived here.'

'It might have looked like this, Laura. Polished within an inch of its life, flowers everywhere, but it never felt like this. It had no heart. You and Derrick, your family, Natasha...'

He stuck his hands in his pockets, stared up at the ceiling, struggling to find words that would convey how they'd transformed this place. Made it somewhere he wanted to come, could walk in and not feel that he was somehow wanting. A want he'd understood when he'd learned the truth. He was a second-best replacement for the boy who'd died in the womb.

There was only one word... 'Love... Love has done this. Your family came together to do this for Natasha because you love her. That's the difference.'

Laura put a sympathetic hand on his arm.

'You're tired, Darius. Working all hours at the foundry and selling a house is as stressful as death or divorce, even when you've only lived there a few years. Four hundred years...' She shook her head. 'I can't begin to imagine how you must be feeling.'

'No...'

He'd had a window, a few hours, and he'd grabbed it,

wanting to be here, to stand by Natasha, but she didn't need him. This was what she'd been working for. The prize. She had everything she wanted.

'Sit down. I'll get you a cup of tea and something to eat. Something to keep up your blood sugar levels. There are cucumber sandwiches, scones, or I've made some Bakewell tarts?'

'Try spiced ginger.'

Natasha was standing in the doorway, flushed, laughing, and his heart leapt as it always did when he saw her. And each time it was different. That first time it had been purely physical, like a rocket going off. The rocket was still there, but now there was so much more. She was so much more. But her laughter, her joy was for something else.

'Well, I'm sure you could do with a break, too,' her mother said, 'so why don't you get it for him while I take the trolley through to the conservatory?'

Natasha walked across the kitchen, sat on his lap, put her arms around his neck and kissed him. 'How are your blood sugar levels now?' she asked, her eyes sparkling, the pulse in her throat thrumming with excitement.

'Up. Definitely up…' he said. 'In fact, this might be a very good time to check out the structural integrity of the boathouse.'

'Tash…' She slid off his lap, tucked a stray strand of hair behind her ear and was four feet away by the time her father appeared in the doorway. 'There's a Mr Darwish asking for you. I've put him in the library.'

'Yikes! Major property buyer.' She stopped at the door, leaned back. 'By the way, we're getting a double page spread in the *Country Chronicle*. Kevin Rose, the editor, knows you are *the* Darius Hadley. I'm afraid you're busted.'

'It was only a matter of time before someone made the connection,' he said. 'Will it help if I talk to him?' he asked, as if he hadn't heard their conversation.

'Darling, if you talk to him we'll be on the front cover.'

'Great,' he said as she flew out of the door. 'I'll do that, then.'

They both watched the space where she'd been for a moment. 'Her career is her world, Darius. She had a bad start in life and maybe we overprotected her.'

'She told me. All of it.'

'She threw up a job that had been her dream to get away. Be independent. Prove something to us.'

'To herself, I think.' That she wasn't that kid lying in a cancer ward, or a basket-case teenager. And she'd done it, becoming the top-selling agent for her company with a bright red BMW sports coupé to prove it. And when she'd been knocked back she'd proved it all over again. 'You knew she turned down the National Trust job?'

He smiled. 'She told you about that too.' He crossed to the fridge. 'I play golf with the man she would have worked for. He asked me why she'd turned the job down—a first, apparently. I never told her mother. Beer?'

'No… Once I've talked to Kevin Rose, I have to get back to London.' She'd given him so much; the least he could do for her was deliver the front page of the *Country Chronicle*. With that very public demonstration of her ability to turn disaster into triumph, she would be able to name her price when she was negotiating terms with Miles Morgan. 'This was just a flying visit. I'm installing a sculpture in Lambourn in a week or two and I had to come down to look at the site.' It was a pathetic excuse by any standards, but Derrick accepted it at face value. 'If I don't manage to catch Natasha before I go, tell her…' What? What could he say? 'Tell her she's better than the best.'

'Darius? Can you talk?'

'If you're quick.'

Tash frowned. Nothing had seemed quite the same between them since the open day. Okay, she'd been busy, he had to be somewhere else, but he'd left without saying goodbye and something was missing. The sex—snatched in brief moments when he wasn't working—was still stunningly hot, but the perfect focus that made her believe that she was the only woman in the world had gone. And those fun 'dates' had been forgotten. It was as if the shutters had come down and she was afraid that the reality of the sale had cut deeper than he'd anticipated. In which case he wasn't going to want to hear this.

Or he was ready to move on. In which case he would.

'I'm working,' he prompted impatiently.

'Yes… Sorry… I just wanted you to know that I've got two firm offers for the house on the table.'

'Two? Are we going to have a bidding war?' He sounded bored rather than excited by the prospect.

'Behave yourself. One is from an overseas buyer who's looking for a small country house to complement his London apartment. He's offering the guide price.'

'Take it.'

'The second offer is lower. I've negotiated them up from their opening bid but it's still half a million below the guide price.'

'So why are we talking about it?'

'Because it's a better package.'

'Can you keep this short? They're waiting to weld the heart in place.'

'Really? You're that close?'

'Natasha, please…'

'Sorry. The second offer is from the IT company across the river. They're expanding and need more space but there are planning restrictions on their own site. The thing is, most of the staff live locally and their children go to the village school so they don't want to move.'

'Then maybe they should up their offer.'

'It's lower, but it's actually worth more. I've managed to exclude the estate cottages, which means you won't have to rehouse the tenants and you'll have more disposable income from the sale. Sitting tenants will also affect the resale value of the properties so it will help reduce the inheritance tax bill. Repairs and maintenance can be offset against tax and the cottages will be realisable assets in the future. Finally—'

'There's more?'

'Finally,' she said, 'they know Gary; he's done jobs for them in the past and they will keep him on as caretaker and odd job man with a salary and company benefits that he could never have hoped to achieve from your grandfather's estate.'

She could have simply presented Darius with the easy offer, job done. They both had what they wanted. House sold, reputation restored and she'd always known that there was no future in this relationship. It wasn't his fault that she'd got four-letter-word involved and she wasn't about to drag it out to the bitter end. Better let go while they were still friends.

But when the first bid had come in from the IT company she'd immediately seen the possibilities—the value to the village, to the people Darius felt responsible for—and she'd hammered out the best deal she'd ever put together. One she would always be proud of. Not only did it ensure that Hadley continued to thrive, but it would keep a link for Darius with the village that bore his name.

'Their surveyor has just left,' she said. 'Say yes and the money will be in the bank by the end of the month.' She waited. 'Hello? Am I talking to myself here?'

'No...' He sounded bemused. 'I'm simply speechless. You are an extraordinary woman, Natasha Gordon. Nothing left to prove. To anyone.'

'Thanks…' Her voice caught in her throat. 'I'll, um, let Ramsey have the details, then, shall I?'

'I suppose so.'

'Darius? Is this what you want? Only if you've changed your mind about selling, tell me now.'

'Why would I do that? Hadley Chase is the last place on earth I'd ever live.'

'I don't know. It's just that you seem a little scratchy.'

'Do I? Why don't you come over and smooth me out?'

Smoothing him out was something she'd taken great pleasure in doing on numerous occasions while he'd been working twelve-hour days, but there was something decidedly off in that invitation. As if he wanted her, but hated himself for it. Or maybe he wanted her to hate him. Whatever it was, all the pleasure drained out of her day.

'I thought you were working,' she said. An alternative to the flat *no* that she knew was the right response. That she couldn't quite bring herself to say.

'You've got me,' he said. And that had sounded like relief.

'I'll call Ramsey now,' she said. 'Get things underway.' He didn't answer. 'Darius? Is this it?'

'Yes,' he said. Abrupt. To the point. 'Job done. Time to think about your fee.'

'The bronze…'

Tash swallowed. No. He'd said it. Job done. And they both knew that they weren't talking about the sale of a house but, after all they'd been through, shared, there was no way she could sit for him like a model being paid by the hour.

'You've done enough. Your interview with Kevin Rose was above and beyond. Do you need any help clearing the house?' she asked. 'There are some lovely pieces of furniture here.' She was sitting at his grandmother's desk and if she could have afforded it she'd have made an offer.

'No. There's nothing there I want. Ramsey will deal with it.'

Nothing? Really? She sat back. Where had the photograph of his mother come from? It could only have been his grandmother. She stroked her hands across the lovely desk. She'd seen one very like it on an antiques programme on the television. That one had had a secret drawer.

Darius stared at the phone for a long time before he hit end call. He'd lied about working. The horse was finished, delivered to the man who'd commissioned it and awaiting positioning in the place where it would forever be leaping over an unseen fence.

He tossed the phone on the sofa where Natasha had sat on the day she'd come to see him, promising him a whole lot more than the sale of his house when she'd looked at him with those big blue eyes and invited him to try her cake.

Senseless. Except that he hadn't lost his senses. He'd found them. Found something he'd never truly known as a boy. Found whatever it was his father had found, because family history suggested that the 'perfect marriage' had been his grandfather's idea. His way of controlling the future.

It was something he'd been running away from as a man, afraid that, like his father, he'd lose himself to something he couldn't control. But he'd been so wrong. You didn't lose yourself; you found yourself in love. Became whole.

He walked across to the clay sculpture that he'd begun the day he drove back from Hadley Chase, knowing that it was over. He'd worked in the foundry in the day, worked on this at night, capturing for ever that moment when she'd reached out to him in her sleep.

He hadn't needed the drawing. His hands had worked the clay, formed the well-known curves, her shoulders, the bend of her knee, her hair tumbled against the pillow.

His fingers curled around the hand extended towards him, that he couldn't see for the tears blinding him.

'Darius...'

'Natasha?'

'I need to see you. Can you spare me half an hour?'

'I'm at the studio. Come over.'

Tash ended the brief call. One last time, she promised herself. One last time.

It was late by the time she arrived at the studio. The studio door stood open and she looked through but the sun was low and the interior was dim. 'Darius?'

He was taking down the photographs of the horse, clearing the decks and, as she hesitated in the doorway, he half turned and it was all still there and more. The heart-leap, the joy, only a hundred times more powerful, underscored by every touch, every kiss, every memory they had made together.

'No cake?' he asked.

'No time,' she said. 'I've been rushed off my feet with work. It's dark in here.'

He flicked a light switch and illuminated the area by his desk, sofa, and she walked across, put down the thick envelope she was carrying.

'More paperwork?' he asked.

'No. I...' This was going to be the last time she saw him and she didn't want it to be like this... 'I was looking at your grandmother's desk and it occurred to me that I'd seen one very like it on an antiques programme. On the television.'

'You're here to tell me that it's worth a fortune?'

'No. I'm here to tell you that it had a secret drawer.'

He became very still. 'That was in it?'

'No, it was empty, but it's what got me looking through the rest of the house. I knew there had to be more than that one photograph. I found this in the attic.'

She opened the envelope, tipped out the contents. Photographs, letters that had come from his parents' flat in Paris. The report of the car accident where they'd died, fleeing across the border with her family. Their death certificates. A letter his father had left for him in case anything went wrong. He'd known the danger...

'I'll leave you to look at them.'

'No!' His hand gripped her arm, holding her there beside him, and he picked up a photograph of his mother holding him in her arms, his father standing beside him with such a look of love on his face that it had brought tears to her eyes when she'd seen it.

And suddenly the stiffness, the self-protective armour melted and she was in his arms, holding him, wiping the tears from his cheeks, murmuring hush sounds as he thanked her.

'Did you ever see your grandfather again?' Tash asked a long time later, after he'd read the letter, looked at the photographs. 'After your grandmother's funeral?'

'That was when Ramsey realised how sick he was. He wouldn't have it, of course, and it was only after a fall and a stay in hospital that we were able to move him into a nursing home for his own safety. I used to go and visit him. Mostly he had no idea who I was; occasionally he thought I was my father and asked me how Christabel was. How long before the baby was due.'

'It's a terrible thing, Alzheimer's,' she said. 'It robs you of the chance to end things properly. Tell people that you love them.'

'Say the words while you can?'

'I...' How could she say yes and not tell him that she loved him? How could she load him with that emotional burden? 'It's complicated.'

'That's what I thought, but I'm going to make it simple.'

He stood up, took her hand and led her across the studio and switched on the floodlights above his work plinth, lighting up a sculpted figure, a scene that was imprinted on her heart.

She took a step closer, looked at herself as Darius had seen her. The figure lying semi-prone amongst a tangle of sheets was sensuous, beautiful, and he hadn't had to reveal her ribs or her organs to show her inner depths. Every thought, every feeling was exposed. Anyone who looked at it would know that this was a woman in love.

The detail was astonishing. In the modelling of the hands, the tiny creases behind the knee, the dimples above her buttocks. They hadn't been in the drawing. He'd done this from memory.

When she turned he was there, watching her.

'She's beautiful, Darius,' she said a little shakily, 'but she's going to be a bit of a tight fit on the mantelpiece.'

'She won't leave here. She's not for display in a gallery window. This was personal, Natasha, for me, an attempt to hold on to something rare, something special. But once it was done I realised that only the real flesh-and-blood woman will do. Tomorrow it will be nothing but a lump of clay.'

'You're going to destroy this?'

'Why would I keep it? Every time I looked at it I'd know what kind of fool I was for sitting back and making a sketch instead of responding to that invitation and getting back into bed with you. For not saying the words. A statue won't laugh with me, cry with me, knock itself out making the world right for me.'

'No.' It could never do that. 'But it will always be perfect. Never grow old. Never demand anything of you—'

'Never give anything back,' he said. 'Never…'

'Never?' she prompted.

'Never love me back.'

He'd said the words as if he was tearing lumps off his flesh.

Not just hot, gorgeous sex but something bigger, something deeper. The one thing that in his privileged youth he'd never known. The one thing that in his successful career he'd never allowed himself.

'Love?'

'The biggest four-letter word in the dictionary,' he said. 'You're right; you should say the words rather than live with regret. I love you, Natasha Gordon, with all my heart. That's it. No claim, no expectation and absolutely no regret.'

Now she was the one with tears stinging her eyes. 'I told myself I didn't want you to feel guilt, Darius, that I wanted you to remember me with pleasure, but I was afraid to put myself on the line… Your courage shames me, you deserve more but I love you, Darius Hadley. With all my heart.' His expression was so intense that for a moment she couldn't speak. Then, never taking her eyes from his, she made a gesture in the direction of the sculpture. 'It's there, on display, for all the world to see.'

For a moment neither of them moved, breathed, and then he kissed her so tenderly, holding her as if she were made of glass. It was a shatteringly beautiful moment, nothing to do with sex, but a promise…

When he drew back, resting his forehead against hers, he said, 'There are a couple of other things I have to say. I need a plus one at the unveiling of the horse next week. The Queen is doing the honours so you'll need a hat.'

She blinked back the stupid tears and began to smile. 'A hat? Right.'

'I've looked up dancing classes but I need a partner. And how do you fancy seeing the new James Bond movie?'

'That's three things.'

'Is that too demanding? Only the thing is, Natasha, I'm looking for more than high-octane no-commitment sex. I'm looking for a grown-up full-time relationship with a woman who knows what she wants—a woman who will have time for me and a family as well as a career. So I'm asking—is that something you can fit around your new job?'

'New job?'

'Didn't hell just freeze over?' he asked. 'I overheard Morgan offer you a partnership.'

And suddenly everything fell into place. 'Is that why you've gone all moody on me?' she asked.

'Moody?'

'Moody, shuttered, closed-up, just like you were when we first met.'

'It's what you wanted.'

'Absolutely.'

'So why didn't you tell me?'

'Maybe because you got all moody, shuttered, closed up,' she said, turning to him on legs that were shaking as she realised how close she'd come to losing this. 'No time for anything but a quickie. Running away. If you'd been talking to me I'd have told you all about it. And that I turned him down.'

'But...' His frown was total confusion. 'You weren't even tempted?'

'I told you, Darius, I could never trust a man who treated me the way Miles did, but it wasn't just that. I like being my own boss. Tailoring my sales pitch to meet individual needs. Looking for the right house for a client who appreciates good service. I like doing things my own way.'

'I like doing things your way, too,' he replied as she began slipping her buttons one by one.

'I have to get up,' Tash protested, making an effort to wriggle out of Darius's warm embrace. 'I've got an appointment at eleven.'

'Where are you going?' he asked, his hand on her belly

spooning her against him as he nuzzled the tender spot behind her ear.

'Sussex. I've found the perfect house for a client and she's flying in from Hong Kong to see it.' She bit her lip as his hand moved lower.

'Is this the one you've been raving about?'

'Mmmm… Can I tempt you to a day out in the country?' she asked in an attempt to distract him. Distract herself. She really, really had to get going… 'Once the viewing is over we could take a walk on the Downs, have lunch at a country pub. Can you spare the time?'

'No,' he said, moving so that she flopped over onto her back and was looking up at him. 'Can you?'

No! The answer was definitely, almost certainly, maybe *nooooo*, but his lips were teasing hers, his hand was much lower and the word never made it beyond a thought.

Damn it, he always did that! She woke in plenty of time to get where she had to be and then he ambushed her. She grinned as her little van pulled out of the mews and she headed south towards the Sussex Downs. It was just as well that she'd started putting the alarm forward half an hour or she'd be permanently late.

As it was, she needn't have worried. She picked up the keys from the selling agent in good time but when she pulled up outside the gates there was no sign of her client, only a voicemail message on her phone saying that she'd been held up, but would she go ahead and take photographs for her of the garden and especially of the grotto.

Terrific. She just hoped it wasn't a wind-up. Over the last few months there had been a few of those—wasted journeys to see non-existent clients, non-existent houses. Rivals who resented the splash of publicity following her sale of Hadley Chase. The feature on her new consultancy in the *Country Chronicle*. She'd got smarter about checking before she wasted time or money on them, but this one had checked out.

She took her camera and her camcorder, filming the walk up the drive to the sprawling house, smothered in an ancient wisteria that would look so pretty in the spring.

It was absolutely perfect—and not just for her client.

There was room for an office, a cottage in the grounds for Patsy—who was working for her now—and Michael. And a small barn tucked away at the rear.

It was a house where two people could grow their lives, their family, and there was no use kidding herself. The only reason she'd wanted Darius to come with her was so that he would see it and fall in love with it too.

The mews cottage was great, but there was no room for an office for her, no room for anything except the two of them indulging in a lot of that high-octane sex. She swallowed. He was the one who'd said he wanted more—commitment, a family.

She didn't need to tour the house to take photographs. She'd done that, leaving them where Darius could see them, hoping… She'd taken a few of the garden but, with a sigh, she set off to take more.

The low sun was gleaming through grasses, scarlet dahlias that were making the most of a lingering autumn. The leaves in the hidden woodland dell that housed a grotto created in the bole of what had once been a huge tree.

She'd seen photographs but hadn't been down there. Today, though, she followed a narrow rill that fell in steps before dropping into a natural stream that trickled into a pool within the grotto. Light was filtering from above and more than just water gleamed in the darkness.

None of this had been in the agent's photographs and, curious, she stepped down. For a moment she couldn't believe what she was seeing and then, as she did, she caught her breath.

It was a bronze of the figure Darius had made, that he'd said he was going to destroy. She was here, lying on a bed, surrounded by a pool—a woodland nymph reaching out for her lover.

She didn't need the tingle at the base of her spine, didn't have to turn around, to know Darius was there with her.

'It's beautiful,' she said.

'Yes.'

She turned. 'How did you know?'

'I didn't. I gave you a description of the house that would be perfect for us. Five bedrooms, room for a home office, an outbuilding of some sort, a staff cottage, and I waited for you to find it.'

'But what about Mrs Harper?'

'There is no Mrs Harper. I'm your client.'

'You? But...' She shook her head. 'But how did you organise this?' she demanded, flinging out a hand in the direction of the sculpture.

'The owner indulged me. Unfortunately, the downside to that was his insistence that it stay, whether we buy or not.'

'But...but...but...' she spluttered. And then she knew. 'You've already bought it, haven't you?'

'It seemed wise, just in case he got a better offer. I've leased out the studio. You decide whether we keep the mews or your flat for our London bolthole; you can find a tenant for the other, which leaves only two questions.'

'Two?'

'The first is: will you marry me?'

She swallowed.

'What's the second question?' she asked.

'I think you'll find that your mother is hoping for a Christmas wedding. Are you happy with that?' He waited as she struggled with a throat that was Sahara-dry. 'If you need a hint, yes and yes are the correct answers.'

She flung herself into his arms, laughing and crying a

little at the same time. 'Yes, and yes, and yes, and yes...'
And then she threw a punch at him. 'You discussed it with
my mother!'

'Let's just say there was some heavy hinting going on
the last time we went for Sunday lunch.'

'Oh, good grief. It's not compulsory, you know!'

'Too late. We've booked the church.' And then he was
kissing her and she said nothing more for a very long time.

Wedding bells, fairy lights glistening over a white frost.
Red berries and ivy twisted around pew ends and around
the Christmas roses in her bouquet. White velvet and her
grandmother's pearls. And Darius.

Darius waiting for her at the altar. Darius holding out
his hand to her, folding it in his and holding on tight, then
smiling as if this was the best day in his life. And Natasha
smiling back because it was the best day of hers. So far.

* * * * *

Mills & Boon® Hardback
March 2014

ROMANCE

A Prize Beyond Jewels	Carole Mortimer
A Queen for the Taking?	Kate Hewitt
Pretender to the Throne	Maisey Yates
An Exception to His Rule	Lindsay Armstrong
The Sheikh's Last Seduction	Jennie Lucas
Enthralled by Moretti	Cathy Williams
The Woman Sent to Tame Him	Victoria Parker
What a Sicilian Husband Wants	Michelle Smart
Waking Up Pregnant	Mira Lyn Kelly
Holiday with a Stranger	Christy McKellen
The Returning Hero	Soraya Lane
Road Trip With the Eligible Bachelor	Michelle Douglas
Safe in the Tycoon's Arms	Jennifer Faye
Awakened By His Touch	Nikki Logan
The Plus-One Agreement	Charlotte Phillips
For His Eyes Only	Liz Fielding
Uncovering Her Secrets	Amalie Berlin
Unlocking the Doctor's Heart	Susanne Hampton

MEDICAL

Waves of Temptation	Marion Lennox
Risk of a Lifetime	Caroline Anderson
To Play with Fire	Tina Beckett
The Dangers of Dating Dr Carvalho	Tina Beckett

0214GEN STD HB